Advanced Dungeons & Dragons 2nd Edition ®

DUNGEON MASTER® Guide

Rules Supplement

The Complete Book of
Villains

by Kirk Botula

Table of Contents

CREDITS

Design: Kirk Botula
Edited: Kevin Stein
Black and white illustrations: Terry Dykstra,
Larry Elmore, Graham Nolan
Color illustrations: Bruce Eagle, Jeff Easley,
Keith Parkinson
Cartography: Dennis Kauth
Typography: Nancy J. Kerkstra
Production: Sarah Feggestad

Thanks to Mark Evans, Mike Schiller, Harvey Coblin,
and Brett Botula.
Special thanks to M.J. for everything.

Virtue untested is innocence.
—Anonymous

TSR, Inc.
POB 756
Lake Geneva,
WI 53147

TSR Ltd.
120 Church End,
Cherry Hinton
Cambridge CB1 3LB

Introduction

Bakshra's Tale

He was called Dog Eater and Priest Hunter. At first we thought the man was our salvation. In the end, he made us fight for the little we had. He's gone, we think, but even now that it's all over, the smell of burning fields and flesh lingers in our dreams and makes it hard for us to sleep at night. His persistent memory suffocates us.

When his horsemen first thundered through the muddy lane of our sleepy hamlet, they were our rescuers. It was as if our darkest thoughts and bitter rage had taken form to protect us from the attacking orc hordes. They cut down our enemies like a farmer threshing his fields, and we prayed for their victory.

As the threat of the orcs diminished, the warriors turned their fury on our people. None realized there would be more to pay for this unholy bargain than just our gratitude. Before it was over, our priests had been burned at the stake and buried in our field. The field has never grown wheat since, and we call it Bakshra's Plain. It was Bakshra, the Dog Eater, who was our undoing.

Overview

This book is intended to help you make your AD&D® game villains nasty, believable, and grandiose. It provides you with practical tools to create unforgettable villains that will make adventures more fun for yourself and your players. In the chapter "Defining Your Villain," we explain how to create a complete and compelling villain. "Henchmen, Flunkies, & Lackeys" describes how to define the individuals who play a minor role in your villain's plots. "Villainous Organizations" looks at the hazards villains create when they band together.

The practical aspects of weaving a plot for your villain are described in the chapter "Introducing Your Villain." The next chapter, "Delivering the Goods," reviews ways of bringing your villain to life through your performance at the game table. The chapter "Monsters into Villains" explains how to turn a MONSTROUS COMPENDIUM® entry into a great villain. The wide variety of unique villains is examined in the chapter

"Advanced Villains." Tools, topics, and techniques that will make your villains more abominable are included in "Creative Villainy." This module ends with a compendium of sample villains, a catalog of ideas for helping to create your own villains, and a series of charts for randomly generating adversaries for your game.

What Is a Villain?

Unlike the friendly innkeepers and livery men who may people your campaign, villains motivate the player characters to action. It is the villain who captures the imaginations of your players and brings them back session after session. A player character may have many foes who are not "real" villains. A villain is more than a random monster or an enemy. Of all the characters who come and go, villains are the most important roles you play as a Dungeon Master.

There are five basic criteria for creating a villain. Let's step through each of the criteria for true villains to discover where they differ from mere enemies. We will find that while all villains are enemies, not all enemies are villains.

1. Villains are opposing forces.

A villain may be an individual or a force of nature. The purpose of a villain in any story is to oppose the heroes and force them to make decisions. Common enemies also share this role as an opposing force to the heroes.

2. Villains are powerful adversaries.

The villain should command more resources than the heroes. The more powerful a villain, the more heroic his defeat.

For dramatic purposes, both enemies and villains alike benefit from playing Goliath to the heroes' David. It is possible to have a vil-lain or enemy who is not very powerful, but such a character would not be much of a challenge to the heroes.

3. Villains are unsympathetic.

Sympathy weakens a villain. The more understanding your characters extend to an opponent, the less fear he creates. The less fear a villain creates, the less danger he poses. The less danger he poses, the less heroic are those who oppose him.

Villains are characters heroes can freely despise. Enemies are sometimes sympathetic. An example of a sympathetic enemy who is not a true villain would be an enemy warrior or a misunderstood monster.

4. Villains have bad motives.

When Robin Hood stole from the rich to give to the poor, he proved that a person can do a bad thing for a good reason. A villain should have bad intentions regardless of whether his actions are considered good or bad.

The very essence of villainy may be bad motives or needs so excessive they are pursued to the detriment of other people. An enemy may have perfectly honest intentions and simply have goals in opposition to those of the heroes.

5. Villain engage emotions.

By giving your players a villain that they love to hate, you will find them coming back to play again and again.

Any game is more exciting if your players care about the outcome of events. To this end, villains, enemies, and even allies should be characters who engage your players' emotions.

By keeping an eye toward these simple rules of thumb, you can create diverse and unique villains to populate your game world.

This chapter takes you through the basic steps to create a compelling villain. Each of the following topics covers one aspect of your villain. We will go through each one and apply it by building a sample villain—Bakshra, the brutal warlord introduced at the beginning of this book. When we have put the finishing touches on our creation, we will interrogate the newly created villain for completeness.

While you can spend hours working up every aspect of a villain's life and personality, you need to know only enough to make the character believable to you. If you have a concise and clear picture of your villain, it is easier to make him come alive for your players.

In this chapter, we will look at each of the following aspects of your villain's life:

1. Occupation
2. Objective
3. Motive
4. Personality
5. Attitudes and behaviors
6. Tastes and preferences
7. Surroundings
8. History
9. Network
10. Appearance
11. Abilities and alignment

As we move through each topic, jot down your own ideas on a piece of paper for a villain of your own creation.

1. Occupation

If we want a believable villain, we need to give him a means of support. What does your villain do for a living? A good place to start when making a villain is to decide how he pays his bills. Simply knowing how a villain supports himself can tell us a great deal about how he spends his time and who he deals with on a daily basis. The first thing we ask when we meet someone is often, "What do you do?"

Many famous villains are known by their occupation. Sweeney Todd, the murderer who killed his victims and served them up in meat pies, was called the "Demon Barber of Fleet Street."

A villain's occupation is sometimes integral to his crimes. Cruella DeVil of *The Hundred and One Dalmatians* was a furrier who was bent upon turning innocent puppies into fur coats. Auric Goldfinger of Ian Fleming's James Bond novel was a gold and jewelry dealer who tried to irradiate the gold in Fort Knox to drive up the value of his own bullion.

Few villains can afford to sit around being villains full time. Batman's enemies always appear with expensive equipment and hide-outs, but we are not expected to really accept these characters as "real."

> Bakshra is a petty warlord who oversees his own castle and is supported by the serfs who work the surrounding farmland.

2. Objective

Your villain's objective should be in direct conflict with those of your heroes. He might want the throne of their kingdom. He might want to destroy one of their friends.

The events and people affected by the villain's actions should be important to the heroes. The players would hardly care if a vicious man spent years in a subterranean catacomb laboring over a stamp collection. However, if he started kidnapping farmers to use as philatelic slaves, you might find your players more interested (and maybe amused).

A villain's occupation may give you ideas regarding your villain's objectives. His plots may extend from his occupational goals. In *Raising Cain*, the villainous child psychologist, Dr. Nix, kidnapped infants in order to conduct experiments on the development of multiple personalities in children.

A villain's objective may also serve a particular story function. For example, you may need to kill a powerful NPC who has begun to throw your game out of balance. In this case, you can make the villain's objective the murder of that NPC.

You may simply want to expose the characters to the culture and hazards of a region in which they have never adventured. Launching a war headed by a villain from this region who has designs on colonizing the PCs homeland may serve this goal.

> Bakshra wants to destroy all religion. He is indiscriminate in his enmity but is particularly dedicated to the destruction of the church and priests that our player characters serve.

3. Motive

What need drives your villain to perpetrate his heinous crimes? In Mark Twain's *The Adventures of Tom Sawyer*, Injun Joe is driven by a need for revenge when he plots against the widow of a judge who had him publicly horsewhipped. Greed motivates Long John Silver to lead a mutiny against the ship captain searching for buried treasure in Robert Louis Stevenson's *Treasure Island*.

A motive is a persistent concern for some goal. In other words, a motive is a need. A "bad" motive is a need pushed to excess and pursued at the expense of other people. Greed can be seen as a desire for security pushed beyond the point of reason.

It is important for your villain to have bad motives. Even if your villain does something nice, it should be for the wrong reason. A ruthless politician may make generous donations to charity to improve his reputation.

Bad intentions are even more important than bad actions. Bad actions are not strictly the province of villains. Robin Hood proved that a person can do a bad thing for a good reason. Even the little old ladies in "Arsenic and Old Lace" who poisoned old men did it out of sympathy for their loneliness. Their good intentions prevent these characters from being villains.

People are motivated by a variety of needs. The most common include:

Achievement

A person with a need for achievement sets out to accomplish difficult tasks. He may maintain high standards and work toward distant goals. An achievement-driven person also likes competition and is willing to put forth more effort to attain excellence.

A villain with an excessive need for achievement may lie, cheat, steal, or kill. Villains may also thrive on the challenge of crushing the heroes.

Affiliation

A person who has a need for affiliation enjoys being with friends and people in general. He accepts people readily. He also makes efforts to win friendships and maintain associations with people.

A villain with a need for affiliation may join a gang of thugs and resort to acts of cruelty to gain their approval.

Aggression

A person with a need for aggression enjoys combat and argument. He is easily annoyed and willing to hurt people to get his way. He may seek to "get even."

A villain with a need for aggression may be a vindictive bully who likes to pick fights, or a tyrant who continually wages war.

Autonomy

A person with a need for autonomy tries to break away from restraints, confinement, or restrictions of any kind. He enjoys being unattached, free from people, places, or obligations, and may be rebellious when faced with restraints.

A villain with a need for autonomy may drift from town to town, conning women into marrying him and eventually running off with their money.

Exhibition

A person with a need for exhibition wants to be the center of attention. He enjoys having an audience and engages in behavior that wins the notice of others. He may enjoy being dramatic or witty.

A villain with a need for exhibition may perform savage acts to gain attention and notoriety.

Safety

A person with a need for safety does not enjoy exciting activities, especially if danger is involved. He avoids risk of bodily harm and seeks to maximize personal safety.

A villain with an overwhelming need for safety would take the only lifeboat on a sinking ship. If the need becomes paranoic, the villain would attack people he believes present a potential threat.

Nurturing

A person with a need to nurture gives sympathy and comfort, assisting others whenever possible. He is interested in caring for children, the disabled, or the infirm, and offers a "helping hand" to those in need. This person readily performs favors for others.

A villain with a twisted need for nurturing might aggravate a sick person's condition or imprison him to make certain the victim remains under the villain's care.

Order

A person with a need for order is concerned with keeping his personal effects and surroundings neat and organized. He dislikes clutter, confusion, and lack of organization. He is also interested in developing methods for keeping materials methodically organized.

A villain with a need for order may run an oppressive totalitarian state that demands conformity from its citizens.

Power

A person with a need for power attempts to control the environment and influence or direct other people. He expresses opinions forcefully. He also enjoys the role of leader and may assume it spontaneously.

A villain with a need for power may murder his superior to advance to a position of greater influence. He may also use magic or psionics to enslave innocent people.

Succor

A person with a need for succor frequently seeks the sympathy, protection, love, advice, and reassurance of other people. He may feel insecure or helpless without such support and confides difficulties readily to a receptive person.

A villain with a need for succor may feed on other people's pity and invent problems to gain comfort. He may stage accidents for money or sympathy. He might be tempted to betray his friends or his country if someone extends him a little sympathy.

Understanding

A person with this need wants to understand many areas of knowledge. He often has a strong intellectual curiosity and values the synthesis of ideas and logical thought.

A villain with a need for understanding may be willing to conduct horrific experiments to satisfy his thirst for knowledge. He may be willing to serve evil entities in exchange for secret knowledge.

> Bakshra has dominating needs for order and power. His lack of spiritual understanding leaves him in a state of internal confusion. He obsessively attempts to impose order on the world around him as if it will somehow help him gain mastery over his own self-doubt and anxiety.

4. Personality

When describing acquaintances to one another we usually associate a person with one or two particular traits, such as, "You remember him. He was that nervous guy who laughed too hard at everyone's jokes." The man's behavior might suggest that he is insecure and seeking the approval of other people. These strong but simple impressions are dominant traits. Fictional characters also have such dominant traits, from the kindly and wise Master Po of the "Kung-Fu" television series to the ambitious and cruel Prince John of the Robin Hood stories. When creating a villain, you should pick two or more dominant traits that serve as your first impression of the character.

The villain's dominant traits should be consistent and reinforce one another. For example, one villain might be reckless and bold, and another might be cowardly and deceitful. However, what often adds interest and makes a villain memorable are the traits which are seemingly contradictory (usually one contradictory trait will be enough to round out a character). This sort of contradictory trait has been used in movies about Nazi Germany in which brutal Gestapo officers are also shown to be loving fathers. Some of James Bond's opponents have had curious interests in gardening or some other hobby which stood in stark contrast to their criminal ambitions.

We can see how a villain's dominant personality traits as well as a contradictory trait are revealed through the conflicts in the movie *Blade Runner*. The villain Roy Batty is the leader of a group of renegade replicants who have returned to Earth. Roy is revealed to be a determined and ruthless mastermind. When he saves the life of a man hired to kill him, we find that Roy has the contradictory trait of compassion.

When building a complete villain, you should define two dominant traits and one contradictory trait, as we shall do now for Bakshra.

Dominant Trait 1: Compulsive
Dominant Trait 2: Discontented
Contradictory Trait: Protective

> Bakshra is compulsive in his efforts to put his spiritual and physical house in order. He is obsessive about his health and appetite.
>
> This obsession with the state of his physical constitution manifests itself in many cold baths, warm glasses of milk, exercise, and an overconcern with drafty rooms. Sturdy as an ox, one would think by watching his behavior that he is in constant fear of his health suddenly failing.
>
> Bakshra is discontented with his inability to achieve peace of mind. His private search for spiritual well-being has been a complete failure, and he is constantly plagued with worry and self-doubt.

5. Attitudes and Behaviors

Determining how our villain regards and treats other people helps decide how to roleplay an encounter when player characters meet the villain. A person's attitudes are not always consistent with his behavior. A snobbish old lady may treat everyone very graciously, but actually feel pity that nobody is as sophisticated as she. A librarian may be imperious with customers but fawning with his superiors. People often treat others differently depending on their relationship and the situation.

There are two important sets of attitudes and behavior to identify for a new character:

1. Attitude toward others
2. Behavior toward others

> Bakshra almost thinks of his soldiers as loyal livestock whom he must shepherd. Although he is suspicious of all outsiders (including his allies), he protects his own men like valuable property.
>
> Bakshra behaves with surprising tolerance toward his men. Some believe that he grants them a tremendous amount of independence. Others perceive his attitude as disinterest. They all agree they are treated far better by Bakshra than they would be in the employ of another warlord.
>
> Bakshra treats outsiders with suspicion. He does not place much value on their lives and, while not inclined to start trouble unnecessarily, he is always happy to end it with his sword.

6. Tastes and Preferences

A villain's tastes and preferences make him more distinctive. Unusual tastes add color and intensity. The young thug Alex of *A Clockwork Orange* had an insatiable appetite for the music of Ludwig van Beethoven. Hannibal Lecter of *Silence of the Lambs* had a taste for human flesh. A villain's tastes can contribute to his villainy or simply make him more distinctive.

> Bakshra is a man of simple stoic tastes. He also has a peculiar preference for eating dog meat. People at the castle swear he began to make a regular habit of the meal in his youth. He dislikes reading and has thrown out most of his library. He enjoys music, and often allows bards to stay at the keep in exchange for several evenings of private entertainment.

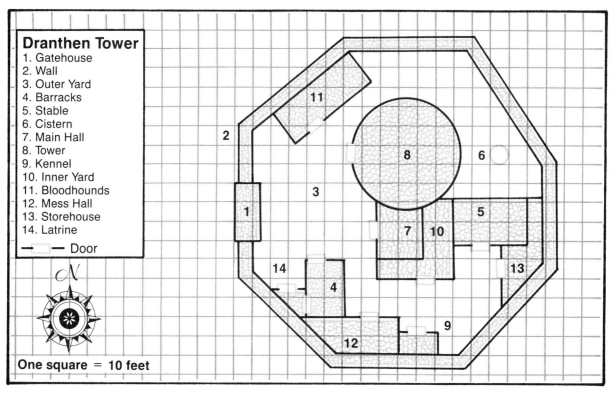

Dranthen Tower
1. Gatehouse
2. Wall
3. Outer Yard
4. Barracks
5. Stable
6. Cistern
7. Main Hall
8. Tower
9. Kennel
10. Inner Yard
11. Bloodhounds
12. Mess Hall
13. Storehouse
14. Latrine

⊏──⊐ — Door

N

One square = 10 feet

7. Surroundings

Define the physical and political surroundings in which a villain lives. The surroundings should be logically consistent with the other aspects of your character's life. Where does your villain live and why? Where does the character tend to go on a daily basis, and how does he get there?

Consider these issues before drawing maps of your villain's environment. These are particularly important questions for DMs who tend to put their villains in a big room at the bottom of a deep dungeon.

Bakshra maintains a walled keep called Dranthen Tower. He lives there with 150 soldiers and a personal staff of 50. Five farming villages in the surrounding area lie under his sway and support an additional 50 soldiers each. His land borders a warlord's domain on one side, orcish territory on another, and independent farmland on the third.

---

8. History

Develop a story explaining the villain's past. A villain's personal history can help explain his motivation and how he became a villain. The term *backstory* is used to describe everything that has happened to your villain prior to entering the adventure at hand.

In James Fennimore Cooper's *Last of the Mohicans*, the cruel Huron Magua grew vengeful when the English killed his family and enslaved him. When Captain James Hook appeared in Barrie's *Peter Pan*, he already had a personal vendetta against the hero for having cut off his hand. Ahab begins Melville's *Moby Dick* obsessively scouring the sea for the whale that bit off his leg.

Gothic horror stories rely heavily on backstory. The process of uncovering the backstory of a place or character is often the protagonists' motivation. Many ghost stories require the heroes to discover a tragedy of the

past to put unsettled spirits to rest. Each of the evil domain lords in the AD&D® RAVENLOFT® setting has a rather dramatic and lurid backstory.

A backstory does not have to involve a dark secret or a melodramatic tale, nor does it need to involve a defining experience which explains the villain's viciousness. It should help you understand your villain's origins. Where did he or she grow up? How did he come to be in his current position? Answering these questions should help you to understand how your villain reacts, as well as the attitudes your villain has toward the world and the people he encounters.

> When Bakshra was a boy, Dranthen Tower was a monastery of an evil cult. Bakshra's father was captain of the monastery's guard. Bakshra inherited his father's strength and hardy constitution.
>
> Bakshra did not value the things which came easily to him, but in frustration chased those things which seemed just out of reach. His discontent led him to seek a life in the dark priesthood of the cult. Seeking a sense of mastery over his own uncertainty, he sought out the priests, who told him that he did not have the talent for spiritual discipline. He once threatened the high priest for withholding secrets. The priest cursed Bakshra with a withering disease.
>
> For the first time, the most stable part of Bakshra's life was in danger. His strength waned and his constitution deteriorated. Bakshra's father, unwitting of the events which precipitated his son's illness, sent for the high priest.
>
> The priest made Bakshra eat raw venison, telling the boy it was his pet dog and the only cure for his disease. In revenge,

> the boy killed the priest, and his father led a revolt and seized the tower.
>
> Bakshra now hates all religions and priests. He hates orcs, too, as he is envious of how they seem at peace with their brutal natures. Tortured by self-doubt, he relies on his intelligence and might to solve problems and enforce order.

9. Network

Who does your villain know? The villain's network is his circle of friends, family, and professional associates or acquaintances in positions of power. A villain's network of associations affects both the heroes' ability to defeat their enemy, and to the resources a villain uses to accomplish his goals.

You may want to flesh out some of your villain's associates in detail. We will describe how to do this in the chapter "Henchmen, Flunkies, & Lackeys." For now, just make notes of the villain's connections; the heroes may use these people to influence the villain.

> Bakshra is part of a loose association of similar lords who have sworn loyalty to a powerful mage named Fallor. The association supports Fallor with soldiers and goods from their estates in exchange for the assistance of the mage and the other lords in times of difficulty.
>
> Bakshra has no immediate family, enjoying the company of his soldiers and an elite order of knights called the Bloodhounds. Bakshra trained the young leader of the militia in a nearby town.

10. Appearance

What is the appearance of your villain? Choose one or two unique physical characteristics by which your players will remember the villain. Traditionally, you could identify villains by their crooked bodies and menacing features which reflect their twisted spiritual state. Extreme beauty has been used to convey the decadence of aristocracy and wealth. The key is to use appearance to individualize a character. Cruella DeVil of *The Hundred and One Dalmatians* is memorable for her hair, which is black on one side and white on the other. She also wears a trademark coat of Dalmatian fur. People still wear Fu Manchu mustaches, named after the evil Chinese villain who made them his trademark.

Stereotypes in appearance are easily avoided if you remember that a person's clothing usually reflects how he perceives himself. Most villains do not think of themselves as villains and are not likely to wear black top hats, cloaks, or whips on their belts.

When considering appearance, you should include:

1. Facial features
2. Typical expression
3. Typical posture
4. Clothing

For Bakshra, we will use the following description:

> Bakshra is a tall, broad-chested, middle-aged man. He has a close-cropped beard and waist-long black hair tied back with a leather thong. His complexion is pale, his forehead broad. His rounded features, unmarred by wrinkles, reveal a certain weariness. His eyes are an unsettling, almost colorless gray.

> Bakshra's posture reflects a degree of exhaustion. While in the castle he usually wears leather pants, boots, and a loose-fitting jerkin; he wears a mail shirt when outside the castle. Bakshra always hangs a scourge from his belt.

11. Abilities and Alignment

The last step of your villain's creation is to define him in game terms. This means building the framework of ability scores, alignment, proficiencies, and class abilities. Use a player character record sheet to record the scores.

Begin by filling in statistics which you may already have in mind. In the case of Bakshra, we know that the villain is an extraordinarily powerful fighter who commands the fear and respect of his minions. We can pencil in a 17 for his Strength and a 16 for his Charisma. We also know that he is a desperately frustrated man who is not at peace with himself or the world. This aspect of his personality might be noted by giving him an unusually low Wisdom of 6. Despite his lack of wisdom, Bakshra is clearly an intelligent man. An above average Intelligence of 13 or 14 might reflect both his cunning and cynicism.

None of Bakshra's remaining attributes have been dictated by the development of his character. We can pencil them in as we see fit or roll them.

When selecting a villain's ability scores, don't pick numbers which make him too powerful. It is usually a character's shortcomings which make them interesting. In Bakshra' case, the needs which grow from his disproportionately low Wisdom are what motivate his villainy.

Bakshra
Human Male
5th Level Fighter

Strength:	17
Dexterity:	9
Constitution:	16
Intelligence:	14
Wisdom:	6
Charisma:	16

Alignment

An important aspect of any character in an AD&D® adventure is his or her alignment. Alignment is often used as a moral and ethical compass to determine a character's direction in various situations. Most villains fall somewhere on the evil side of the fence; however, a non-evil alignment may be appropriate depending upon the alignment of your player characters. Remember, your villain should exist in opposition to your heroes as much as possible. We will examine the issue of alignment in more detail in the section on "Creative Villainy." For now we will continue with our example.

Bakshra is lawful evil, but he does not perceive himself as evil. He is a man of his word even in his dealings with his enemies. It is this obsessive and ruthless adherence to rules that he sees as virtuous. He is, as mentioned earlier, a cynical man. He thinks of himself as above questions of good and evil.

Abilities

A person's abilities are an important part of their identity, and in weakly defined characters, often becomes a substitute for depth. This is particularly true of comic book superheroes who have extraordinary talents but no personality. A strength of the AD&D® rules lies in the clear system for defining a character's abilities.

Even if you do not use the nonweapon proficiency rules, it can be helpful to roll or select some for your villain. It provides one more way to round out your character.

Nonweapon Proficiencies: carpentry, stonemasonry, tracking

Bakshra developed skill in carpentry and stonemasonry when he spent his youth helping to build and maintain the walls of his father's stronghold. His ability has bolstered his paranoia, and his castle is riddled with false walls, secret passages, and deadly traps. He also spent much of his free time with his favorite dog, tracking small game in the surrounding hills. He now uses this talent to make a game of hunting priests who wander into his territory.

Weapon Proficiencies: awl pike, bastard sword, dagger, horseman's mace, scourge

Bakshra served as a soldier in the monastery prior to the fall of the priests, when he learned to wield a pike and dagger. He trained with a bastard sword upon becoming an officer. As captain, he adopted the horseman's mace when mounted. He uses a scourge to interrogate prisoners.

Increasing the Intensity

The last step in drawing up your character is to push him beyond everyday boundaries, allow him to become excessive: Take what should be a well-rounded believable character and unbalance him. Try to add the element that ultimately distinguishes your villain from all the rest. It isn't as hard as you might think.

1. Give your character a twist.
2. Take an existing attribute and exaggerate it.

We know Bakshra has an intense enmity for priests. Let's give it a twist. Suppose that, unknown to his men, Bakshra maintains a small chapel in his castle where he secretly labors to master the disciplines of the clergy. His failures fuel his bitterness toward the priesthood.

Now let's exaggerate an already bizarre trait of our villain. We established in the section on "Tastes and Preferences" that Bakshra makes a habit of eating dog meat. His backstory suggests that this may be related to the lie of the high priest who healed him in his youth. Perhaps Bakshra never knew that the priest had lied about curing his curse with his dog. Perhaps he has continued to make a ritual of the meal in order to ward off any power that a priest's magic might gain over him, and additionally serve as a constant reminder of his anger. What if Bakshra breeds a huge number of beautiful hounds and travels far and wide in search of rare and unique dogs? He is never seen traveling without a pack of hounds, and he makes a meal of one of his dogs every night.

Reviewing the Process

We have moved through the process of defining a complete villain. We explained each of the basic components of a believable character and eventually distilled the villain into a set of statistics, allowing us to bring the villain into the game.

You can draft a villain into your AD&D® game in two ways. You can start writing or start rolling; that is, you can literally design a complete villain on paper without ever touching a die, or you can begin by rolling ability scores. Each approach has its advantages, and you can easily use a combination of these two methods by rolling some attributes and filling in others.

Rolling up your villains forces you to think creatively and helps prevent you from falling into ruts; it can also overwhelm you with information, making it somewhat difficult to get a clear initial picture. However, drafting your villains on paper without recourse to dice can be risky—villains can begin to seem alike.

There are two rules to follow when drawing up a villain. If you know what you want, write it—don't roll it. Secondly, if you want a better chance of genuinely surprising yourself, roll it and try to make sense of the numbers.

The steps required to create a complete and well-rounded villain are not necessarily sequential. There are as many ways to approach the process as there are interesting villains who have emerged from it. We have followed a particular thread in creating Bakshra, but you might choose a completely different angle of approach. If you consider each of the topics, you will have a complete villain who is ready to play a crucial role in your adventure.

Fleshing Out Your Villain

When you have difficulty fleshing out a character, keep a few things in mind:

1. Look at Disparities

When developing a character's personality traits or motivation, look at disparities in the ability scores. A weakness can create a need, while an unusual strength might result in overdependence.

2. Create Interest through Contrast

Whether you are dealing with a character's personality or developing his surroundings, contrast and tension always draws attention.

3. When in Doubt, Roll a Die

Even if you do not intend to use randomly generated information, it is sometimes easier to modify something to your liking than to draw it up from scratch.

4. When You Are Convinced, Stop

When the villain is believable to you, avoid burdening the character with unnecessary detail. Allow the villain room to grow during the course of the game.

Interviewing Your Villain

This section provides a series of questions to help you get a clear picture of your villain. Once you have worked through the previous steps, these questions serve as a final check of your villain's completeness.

Occupation

What do you do for a living?
Why did you choose this vocation?

Objective/Motive

What are you trying to do?
Why are you trying to do that?
How do you measure your degree of success or failure?
What will you do if you gain your goal?
What will you do if you fail?
What do you consider the greatest obstacles to your success?
What are you doing to ensure that you overcome these obstacles?
If you could change one thing about the world, what would that be?
If you could change one thing about yourself, what would that be?
Do you fear anything?

Personality

How would others describe you?
How would you describe yourself?

Attitude

Are there any individuals you trust or rely on?
Are there any individuals who trust or rely upon you?
Do you enjoy the company of others or do you prefer to be alone?
Do you have servants or employees? How do you gain their cooperation?
Are you a servant or employee? How does this relationship benefit your personal interests?

Tastes and Preferences

How do you spend your leisure time?
What do you like to wear?
What do you enjoy most about your work?
What do you like to eat?
Do you collect anything?
Do you have any pets?

Surroundings

Where do you live?
What is the climate?
Why do you live there?
What political boundaries lie near your home?

The Complete Villains'
Worksheet

Name: _____

Class: _____

Alignment: _____

Occupation: _____

Objective: _____

Motive: _____

Dominant Trait 1: _____

Dominant Trait 2: _____

Contradictory Trait: _____

Attitudes and Behavior s: _____

_____

_____

_____

Tastes and Preferences: _____

_____

_____

Surroundings: _____

_____

_____

History: _____

_____

_____

_____

_____

_____

_____

_____

Network: _____

_____

_____

Appearance: _____

_____

_____

What natural resources exist in the area?

What resources are scarce?

What is your daily routine?

What is interesting about the population in your area?

How do you protect your home? Could you be trapped there in the event of fire or intrusion?

History

What is your name?

How old are you?

Where were you born and raised?

Did you know your parents?

How do you feel about them?

Are your parents alive?

How did your parents make their living?

Do you have any brothers or sisters? If yes, do you know where they are?

What role did your family play in your upbringing? If they did not play a significant role, who did and in what respect?

Did you have any friends in your youth?

Are you married? If yes, what do(es) your spouse(s) do for a living?

Do you have any children? How many? What ages?

What is your race?

Did you receive formal education?

How did you learn to do what you are doing now?

What has been your greatest achievement?

What has been your greatest disappointment?

Network

Who are your influential acquaintances?

Who are your personal enemies?

Who do you interact with on a daily basis?

Appearance

What do you look like?

What aspect of your physical appearance is most distinctive or easiest to identify you?

Abilities and Alignment

What is your religion?

What are your most developed skills?

What are your least developed skills?

Getting Ideas

So your player characters finally defeated your incredible villain. Its been weeks since they beat him, and they still talk about him. Now what do you do to follow up? There are many times when you might find yourself at a loss for ideas for a new villain.

Fortunately, there are great sources for ideas all around us. Whether you are inspired by a person in the news, a character in a book, or your own imagination, you are never at a loss for a villain for long.

Life

Pick up any newspaper, take a walk down any street, and odds are good you will find an idea for a villain. Don't try to lift someone's personality from real-life. While real life villains are certainly believable (mostly), they are not necessarily very interesting, and they are not likely to be a villain of the grand and terrible type that you want for your game.

However, just like writing a book or movie, you can get the kernel of an idea for a story from the newspaper. A mysterious incident can trigger an idea for a plot, or a public enemy might inspire a game villain.

Fiction

Books can also provide ideas. Many of the examples in this book were drawn from novels, movies, television, and comic books. Find any story with a hero, and you are likely to find a villain skulking nearby.

Dice-Rolling

As suggested earlier, a great way to create a fresh villain is to roll his characteristics randomly. Nothing challenges a creative mind like trying to make sense of random figures. Even if a randomly generated character gives you only the spark of an idea, you can keep what you like and discard the rest.

Developing Your Idea

Once you have a kernel of an idea, run it through the process described at the beginning of this chapter and the villain will take shape. All you need to get started is one component of your villain. You can usually deduce the rest of the character from that.

Bakshra was created from a randomly generated set of ability scores. We decided to make him a fighter because we thought too many villains are spellcasters. Then, looking at the numbers, we asked, "What would a guy with no wisdom but a decent intelligence be like? And what if he desperately wanted wisdom? In fact, what if he wanted to be a cleric?"

It doesn't take much to get started.

Henchmen, Flunkies, & Lackeys

No man is an island, and no villain would be complete without lackeys, henchmen, partners, overbearing mothers, and mentors in crime. We have already addressed the idea of a villain's network of associates. This section shows how to create these minor characters. We will create two sample minor characters to support Bakshra.

You should take the time to generate the key people who may become embroiled in your adventure. These are probably the ones your villain relies upon or works with daily. These minor characters may be the first contacts your heroes have with the villain. Supporting characters may take the form of employees, friends, neighbors, business associates, mentors, rivals, and even enemies.

Minor characters should be less complex than the villain. If they are too interesting, they draw attention away from the villain. Restrict minor characters' personalities to their two dominant traits. Develop them further only if the story demands. You might have to roll up some hit points or spells if they actually fight your player characters.

Relationships

At this point, you know enough about your villain to draw conclusions about the people with whom he surrounds himself. The villain should almost always have the stronger personality of any relationship in which he is involved. Here are two easy rules of thumb to follow when designing supporting characters:

Opposites Attract

This is one stereotype which can be helpful in designing relationships for your villains. This is not to be construed to mean that your evil characters will surround themselves with do-gooders. Think again of your villain's dominant traits. People are often attracted to others who have traits they lack but value highly. A scatterbrained person may seek an extremely well-organized assistant. A bully might like to be surrounded by weaklings.

Likes Attract

This rule may hold true even more than the previous rule. We all enjoy and seek out the company of like-minded peers. Our bully might enjoy drinking with other bullies and trading stories about how they each bully people. Of course, such relationships based upon contrast or tension are more interesting than those based on commonalties. As in a photograph, contrast always heightens the definition and clarity of the things we see.

Why Do I Need You?

The supporting characters exist for two specific reasons. The first reason is the villain's need for associating with the minor character, and the second is the minor character's reason for associating with the villain. These reasons may be practical, such as a villain's need for a cook, or they may be both practical and emotional, such as a villain who not only needs a cook, but whose relationship with his flattering cook fulfills his need for approval from others.

Use these four needs to structure the relationships between the villain and the supporting character:

1. Villain's practical need
2. Villain's emotional need
3. Supporting character's practical need
4. Supporting character's emotional need

Interesting relationships can be created by varying the level of fulfillment for each of these needs. For example, a villain may have a wife who serves the practical functions of "a wife in the community." The respectability associated with the marriage, as well as the ability to contribute to raising a family, may all serve the villain's practical need. Emotionally, the villain may find the relationship unsatisfying. In turn, the wife may feel that her emotional expectations are fulfilled, but that the villain does not meet the practical needs. The villain may have an awful reputation, diminishing the esteem of the wife in the community.

Interesting situations can arise when a minor character is an enemy of the villain. This is not to say that the character will be an ally of the player characters, but that he is a force which could work against or alongside the PCs. For example, one of Bakshra's fellow warlords might find himself personally opposed to Bakshra, allying with him only out of desire to keep the villainous organization intact. Cunning PCs might convince this warlord to assist them in destroying Bakshra; if such an overture is mishandled, the PCs could find themselves with a new enemy.

The following are two minor characters close to Bakshra. The first is a like-minded soldier who might serve as a hook for the player characters. The second character may prove to be Bakshra's undoing. You need to worry about game statistics only if it appears your player characters are going to fight with these minor characters.

Supporting Character Record Sheet

Name: _____ Class: _____ Level: _____

Alignment: _____ Gender: _____

Dominant Trait 1: _____

Dominant Trait 2: _____

Villain's Practical Need: _____

Villain's Emotional Need: _____

Supporting Character's Practical Need: _____

Supporting Character's Emotional Need: _____

Description of Relationship: _____

_____

_____

_____

_____

_____

_____

Notes and Statistics: _____

_____

_____

Panden

A former soldier trained under Bakshra, Panden left to become captain of the militia in a neighboring independent farming community. Panden offers a way for the player characters to meet Bakshra.

Dominant Trait 1: Responsible
Dominant Trait 2: Perfectionist

1. Villain's practical need: Always needs good soldiers
2. Villain's emotional need: Affiliation—the need for the company of like-minded people
3. Supporting character's practical need: Needed a job
4. Supporting character's emotional need: Achievement and Affiliation—the need for approval of a superior

Panden worked for Bakshra, and the two struck up an unusual friendship. Despite Bakshra's tendency to be emotionally distant, he responded to Panden's diligence and refusal to compromise the quality of his work. Panden admired similar traits in his employer. However, he always found talking to Bakshra awkward and became uncomfortable with the older man's attention.

Panden and Bakshra's relationship is amicable, though they only speak once or twice a year. Bakshra has made it clear that an opportunity awaits Panden at Dranthen Tower if he ever tires of country life. Panden's need for achievement led him to accept his current job.

Andrea, Priestess of Anthara

A captive of Bakshra, Andrea may eventually betray her captor or cause him to change his course. She is the one person whom Bakshra would like to please.

Dominant Trait 1: Nurturing
Dominant Trait 2: Lackadaisical

1. Villain's practical need: Wants to learn clerical magic
2. Villain's emotional need: Understanding—the need for a sense of spiritual well-being
3. Supporting character's practical need: None—she is a captive
4. Supporting character's emotional need: Nurturing—the need to tend to the weak

Andrea is a chaotic good priestess captured by the Bloodhounds. She was to be released for a hunt but caught Bakshra's attention with her disarming manner. Rather than grovel, plead for her life, or curse her captors, she seemed amused by the incident. Irrepressibly impish, the mischievous priestess was alternately sympathetic and playfully teasing toward Bakshra.

Bakshra originally attempted to break Andrea's spirit, but became intrigued by her good-natured strength. He has made her custodian of his chapel and charged her with teaching him spiritual mastery. She has been entirely unsuccessful in this task, but is not particularly concerned. Her presence in the tower is unknown to Bakshra's men, who believe he killed her personally.

When we cornered him, we knew we would never take him alive. He was one of the Bloodhounds, Bakshra's warrior elite. He stared at us, keeping us at bay with his outstretched sword. Our priest moved to the front of the party to help subdue the warrior. Upon seeing him, the Bloodhound suddenly dropped his sword and knelt in surrender. We were surprised that he would let us take him alive.

When our cleric moved toward him, the man leapt and tried to bite open the priest's throat. The two wrestled until we could pull the knight off the stunned cleric. He had let us capture him because he believed there was a chance he might kill our priest.

The man was a fanatic.

This section builds upon the villain creation tools to develop corrupt organizations. Villainous organizations can provide years of adventures as your heroes defeat individual villains within the organization, who are then replaced by more loathsome villains. The Cold War inspired hundreds of imagined evil organizations, many of which were assembled for the sole purpose of perpetrating villainy. James Bond combated SPECTRE (Special Executive Command for Terrorism, Revenge, and Extortion). Lancelot Link spent his career dedicated to the destruction of CHUMP. Faceless corporations and renegade government agencies have been favorite villains in many movies. In role-playing games, secret cults, tyrannical armies, and guilds of thieves have all been assembled to test the heroes' mettle.

There are two types of evil organizations commonly encountered in role-playing adventures:

1. The hierarchy
2. The network

We will review each of these forms, and see how best to build and maintain such organizations over the life of your campaign.

The Hierarchy

From enemy armies to evil churches, villainous hierarchies are found in some of the most memorable adventures. Hierarchies are organized by rank or authority. Large hierarchies are often characterized as bureaucracies. The very word conjures images of inefficiency and suffocating conformity.

Bureaucracies have the following traits:

1. Specialization

Each lackey within a bureaucracy does one particular job and knows little about activity outside his area. This can make it tough for PCs to extract information from an ignorant flunky. Specialization is often used by secretive organizations, such as terrorist groups.

2. Standard Procedures

Everything is done the same way again and again. This tendency of bureaucracies is helpful to PCs when trying to learn some regular activity of the villainous organization, such as when guards change duty.

3. Office Independent of Individual

People can be easily substituted or replaced because authority lies in titles and positions, not individuals.

4. Inflexibility

Bureaucracies are not well prepared to innovate or respond quickly to a changing environment.

5. Dominance of Authority

Everyone has a boss to step on his head and a lackey beneath to step on in turn. Additionally, the accumulation of power, as well as its exercise, is a goal in itself. This is helpful when threatening or bribing organization men, since they willing to find ways to increase their own power at the expense of their superiors. Subordinates are inclined to follow orders blindly.

6. Position Protection

Rather than rise by merit, people tend to advance within the organization by length of employment. These people exert their time and resources protecting their positions, regardless of whether it is in the best interests of the organization.

Creating an enemy organization rife with red tape and inefficiency creates the illusion that the organization seems less likely to mobilize itself effectively against the heroes. However, there are two important reasons why a bureaucracy can be a dangerous force. The first is the organization's literal power; even the most incompetent general's army can create a formidable threat by doing nothing more than mustering superior numbers. The corrupt bureaucracies of the sorcerer-kings in the AD&D® DARK SUN® world of Athas become much more dangerous when their templars have the power to indiscriminately throw citizens into prison and kill spellcasters on sight.

The second weapon of the bureaucracy is the professional.

The Professional

The professional operates independently to accomplish the goals of the organization. James Bond was a professional working for the bureaucratic British Secret Service. Darth Vader was a professional working for the bureaucracy of the Empire. In a fantasy setting, a professional within a bureaucracy may be a wizard who is counselor to a king, or holy assassin of a church. The professional can work quickly and independently, but can also draw upon the greater resources of the hierarchy which backs him. Professionals make good villains.

The Network

In contrast to the clumsy but powerful hierarchy, the network acts as "grapevine." Networks regularly change their structure and form. It is possible for networks to cross the boundaries of bureaucracies, and they can trace lines of communication and influence from one organization to another.

There are usually few layers of authority between the bottom and the top of a network's organization. However, there may be a number of individuals comprising each of those layers, and the highest level of the organization is likely to be a small group rather than an individual. Villainous networks often appear in the form of black markets and bands of smugglers.

Here are several other significant differences between hierarchies and networks:

Power and Authority

In a bureaucracy, power is concentrated at the top, as opposed to a network, which tends to have small islands of influence. Conse-

quently, an enemy general issues orders meant to be followed without question; a black marketer may need to jockey for advantage with his buyers and suppliers.

Networks often serve only as a means of communication and do not initiate actions. Decisions are made by committees, and these committees take longer to arrive at decisions than the direct chains of command in a hierarchy. However, hierarchies can be as slow as a network when a committee lies at the top of a chain of command.

Communication

Word generally travels faster and more accurately in a network than in a bureaucracy. Documents, letters, and written orders are usually accurate in a bureaucracy, while word of mouth tends to be unreliable. Written communication in networks is only marginally accurate because messages tend to go through several channels before being committed to paper.

Commitment and Satisfaction

Members of a bureaucracy are less committed to the organization's decisions than members of a network. Job satisfaction is usually much lower in a hierarchy. An example of this dissatisfaction is the Soviet bureaucracy's supposed dedication to the destruction of capitalism. The high-ranking Soviet officials spurned these objectives and enjoyed black market western goods, while the lower-echelon bureaucrats often accepted bribes for political favors.

Building Villainous Organizations

Just like building an individual villain, there are a number of traits which you need

The Hierarchy vs. the Network

	The Hierachy	The Network
Power & Authority	Concentrated at the top	Small islands of influence throughout
Communication	Slower but more accurate	Faster but less accurate
Commitment & Satisfaction	Less personal involvement	Greater independence, greater commitment

to define when you create a villainous organization. We will discuss each of the components you should consider before allowing your villainous group to unleash its fiendish conspiracies upon your world. As we continue, we will define a sample villainous organization called the Bloodhounds, a hierarchical order of knights who serve Bakshra in persecuting the clergy. At the end of this section, we will review the process by defining another villainous organization, the Fallorian Alliance, a network of evil warlords, of which Bakshra is a member.

We will build our villainous organization by answering the following questions:

What do they deliver?
How do they acquire resources?

How are they organized?
Do they have an advantage?
How do they plan for the future?
How do they establish conformity?
How do they satisfy their audiences?
Who are the prominent characters?

What Do They Deliver?

This is similar to the objective of an individual villain. You need to define the goods or services the organization provides, as well as how this serves the interests of the participants. An evil church may provide a place of worship for its cultists and provide a path to power for its priests. A network of smugglers might a variety of contraband for the mutual benefit of the suppliers and buyers.

> The Bloodhounds are an elite unit of knights who serve Bakshra without question. Their sole purpose is to rid his territory and the neighboring lands of all priests and religions.

How Do They Acquire Resources?

Any team needs access to the training, materials, and tools of their trade. For the evil church, this may take form as recruiting efforts to locate young priests, or collections conducted to raise funds. The network of smugglers would need a contraband supply, safe houses for hiding out, transportation for their cargo, and contacts in the black market for resale of their goods.

> The Bloodhounds are supported entirely by Bakshra. When traveling, they have the right to requisition any resources needed from the citizens of Bakshra's domain.

How Are They Organized?

For role-playing purposes, you will need to know the structure of the organization, how power is distributed, and how activities are coordinated. The evil church may take the form of a hierarchy, with a high priest at the top and lowly acolytes at the bottom. Smugglers avoid operating the same way twice; they are probably a small committee of thugs, corrupt businessmen, and city officials who beg, borrow, and steal to make certain their goods flow freely.

> The Bloodhounds are organized as a rigid hierarchy. A single captain has sole decision-making authority. Two men report directly to the captain. There are four ranks of knights, and every knight serves as a squire to the knight immediately above him in rank. The lowest ranking knights have "true" squires serving them. There are only 15 Bloodhounds.

Do They Have an Advantage?

A band of villains must overcome competition to survive over time. Using fewer resources, or delivering a service or product no one else provides ensures the long life of an organization. An evil church may be able to summon more power from their foul god than the good church down the road. The network of smugglers may have the head of the border patrol on their payroll, ensuring that their shipments make it across the lines while other would-be smugglers are stopped and harassed.

> The Bloodhounds disregard all laws but their own.

How Do They Plan for the Future?

Outside events can threaten a villainous organization that is not prepared to respond to change. An evil church might stockpile magic and weapons for a holy war to eliminate its competition. Smugglers might expand the types of contraband in which they deal, in case another supplier appears or the queen decides to legalize their wares.

> The Bloodhounds' only concern is to execute their master's will and perpetuate their order. Squires are trained to ensure that 15 knights always ride together. When a Bloodhound is so wounded or aged that he cannot fight, he is torn apart by his comrades.

How Do They Establish Conformity?

Villainous organizations try to maintain consistency in their people and processes. The evil church may have a school to indoctrinate its members, and ancient rituals to ensure certain procedures are perpetuated. It may regularly send priests into the villages to perform healing for a standard fee, ensuring that people know when and where to use this service. The network of smugglers may have its own rituals and tests for indoctrination, and always use certain codes to mark drop-off spots.

By their nature, networks are much less conformist than bureaucracies.

> The Bloodhounds adhere to a strict code of behavior which they regard with cult-like reverence. The code regulates their behavior including eating, sleeping, and combat. Only the captain may sanction a breach of observance. Failure to adhere to the code may result in punishments ranging from ritualistic scarring to death.

How Do They Satisfy Their Audiences?

Every villainous organization has several audiences, including lackeys, financiers, and patrons. A balance must be struck to meet the needs of these diverse groups to gain their continuing support. The evil church may need to provide healing services to the neighboring towns to build an atmosphere of tolerance. It may also need to pander to the king to avoid harassment or inordinate taxes. The network of smugglers must provide adequate returns to investors and pay off the flunkies who do the dirty work.

> The Bloodhounds have only two constituencies: themselves and Bakshra. The warlord is pleased with the obsessive order of knights, and with their unquestioning and effective service. The knights themselves are immersed in their own mythology. They live only to serve. The knights have become even more fanatical about Bakshra's desire to wipe priests from the earth than Bakshra himself. If there is ever a conflict regarding this issue, the knights are likely to rebel.

Who Are the Prominent Characters?

When you first establish a villainous organization in your campaign, you should define the members who set the objectives. Additionally, you need to keep track of any "bit players" encountered by the adventuring party. These minor functionaries can be summarized by a few notes. Other characters require more complete development. In our examples, we abbreviate alignments.

> **The Bloodhounds**
> There are 15 Knights and 16 squires.
> Elgin, captain of the Bloodhounds: LE, male human, 6th level fighter.
> Typical Bloodhound: LE, human, 5th level fighter.
> Typical squire: LE, human, 3rd level fighter.

The Fallorian Alliance

Having stepped through the process of defining a villainous hierarchy, we will use the same procedure to create a network of villains.

What Do They Deliver?

The Fallorian Alliance is a network of warlords. The Alliance provides security to its members and the aid of a powerful wizard. Bakshra is a member of this network.

How Do They Acquire Resources?

Each member of the Fallorian Alliance makes his resources available to other members threatened by outside forces. In other words, if a member is attacked, all the other members must contribute soldiers. If a member suffers a famine, all the other members must contribute food. This close relationship also makes it easier to evaluate the potential for treachery.

Each lord is responsible for supplying a tenth of his revenue to the Alliance. This amount is held in trust and is used for spell research by the mage Fallor. These funds are also used when the joint interests of the Alliance are threatened.

How Are They Organized?

The Fallorian Alliance consists of six warlords; each member has an equal vote. Fallor does not have a formal vote and is regarded as a resource of the committee. In reality, the mage provides significant counsel regarding all group decisions. A warlord is free to run his own affairs as long as his business does not interfere with the other members' dealings.

Do They Have an Advantage?

The pooling of resources has enabled the Fallorian Alliance to benefit from Fallor's research in ways that none would have managed individually.

How Do They Plan for the Future?

As a group, the Fallorian Alliance is interested in maintaining a balance of power. They support the status quo and encourage Fallor's research. However, some members of the Alliance are concerned about Fallor's growing power, afraid that the mage could grow too powerful for the Alliance to control.

How Do They Establish Conformity?

The Fallorian Alliance adheres to principles of disclosure and mutual aid. Members meet twice a year to discuss concerns. They use Fallor to detect dishonesty in the meetings. Recently, Fallor accused a member of lying, and the man was executed by the Alliance (who divided his holdings among themselves). This established a bloody precedent.

How Do They Satisfy Their Audiences?

The only groups served by the Alliance are Fallor, the members, and the people living within the domain of each member. Fallor is quite pleased to have his personal research subsidized, which will continue indefinitely as long as he occasionally produces something of value to the Alliance.

> The warlords have security against outside enemies without the additional burden of supporting massive armies. They also have security against the treachery of their Alliance neighbors who might, under different circumstances, be adversaries. The citizens of the various domains benefit from the relative state of peace within the borders of their homelands.

Who Are the Prominent Characters?

> **The Fallorian Alliance**
> Fallor, NE, male human, 10th level magic-user.
> Bakshra, LE, human, 5th level fighter.
> Kazbar, LN, female human, 7th level fighter. (Kazbar thinks Bakshra is a nut.)
> Pastral, LN, female human, 4th level thief. (Pastral is the Alliance messenger.)
> Cooldoom, NE, male half-elf, 8th level fighter. (Cooldoom wants to dominate the entire Alliance.)
> Barkus, LE, male human, 6th level fighter. (Barkus considers Bakshra a good friend.)
> Ramey, LE, female human, 5th level fighter.
> Ferrin, LE, male human, 6th level fighter.

Good People in Bad Places

One of the wonderful aspects of an organization is its ability to acquire its own life. It is quite possible for an organization made up of well-meaning individuals to perpetrate widespread destruction.

Anytime an organization becomes so large that one person cannot understand all its activities, two events occur. First, informal islands of influence and power develop within the formal structure that pursue agendas at odds with the organization. Second, organization members lose any sense of personal responsibility for the unanticipated negative consequences of the organization's actions. At this point, the organization can go out of control.

It is also possible for "good" individuals to become potential allies to the PCs within a villainous organization. A group run by a villain may not require that members have the same alignment as the villain. In fact, it is likely that a villain will staff an organization with lawful neutral employees, unless the organization is a religious group. These lawful neutrals will do their work responsibly without questioning the moral aspects of their jobs.

The Tide of Time

Organizations can survive the defeat of any single villain within its ranks. If the heroes burn the chapter house of a notorious thieves' guild and capture its leaders, it may only be a matter of months before surviving members regroup and seek revenge. Like NPCs, organizations are much more interesting if they change over time.

As you introduce your villainous organizations to your campaign, keep track of individuals in the organizations encountered by the heroes and the outcome of the encounter. This makes it easier for you to predict an NPC's next reaction to the player characters.

Management

In general, hierarchies are inflexible and networks have slow response times. Bureaucracies are best for accomplishing specific tasks; organization falters when a bureaucracy encounters change or a new situation. Networks take longer to make decisions, though they can easily make decisions on any

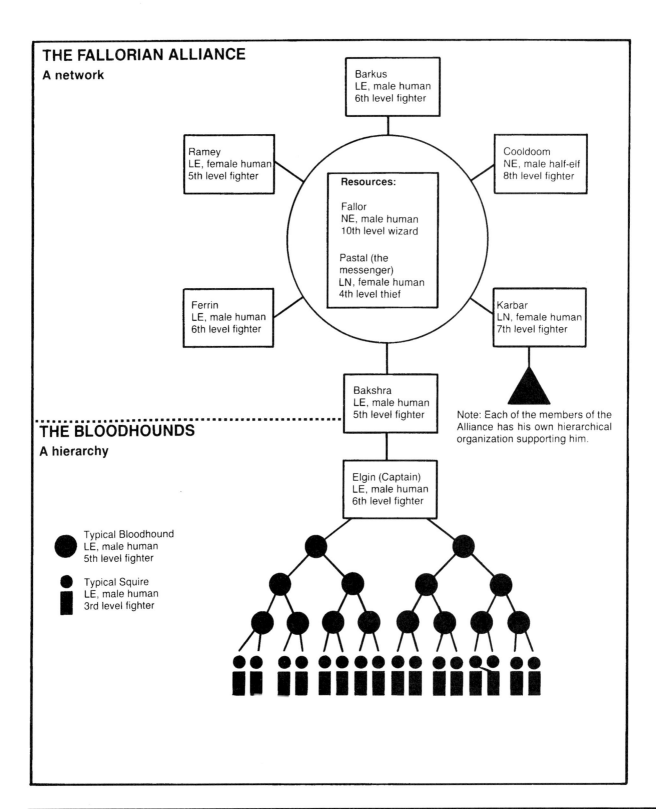

THE FALLORIAN ALLIANCE
A network

Barkus
LE, male human
6th level fighter

Ramey
LE, female human
5th level fighter

Cooldoom
NE, male half-elf
8th level fighter

Resources:

Fallor
NE, male human
10th level wizard

Pastal (the messenger)
LN, female human
4th level thief

Ferrin
LE, male human
6th level fighter

Karbar
LN, female human
7th level fighter

Bakshra
LE, male human
5th level fighter

Note: Each of the members of the Alliance has his own hierarchical organization supporting him.

THE BLOODHOUNDS
A hierarchy

Elgin (Captain)
LE, male human
6th level fighter

Typical Bloodhound
LE, male human
5th level fighter

Typical Squire
LE, male human
3rd level fighter

topic regarding their goals.

To simulate the inflexibility of a hierarchy, maintain a list of specific tasks for which your organization has established standard procedures. Thereafter, when forced to perform a new action, someone in the bureaucracy (probably one of your pregenerated flunkies) must make an Intelligence check. Failure means a delay of one combat round or one turn (depending on the situation) before another check can be made. The organization either acts in the manner in which it has been trained, or does nothing until the decision-maker succeeds the Intelligence check. This penalty does not apply to professionals.

For example, if the guards of a merchant fort are not specifically trained to respond to escape attempts by prisoners, they will not perform well when the PCs make a prison break. Consequently, the commander of the guard must make an Intelligence check before trying Tracking checks or requesting help from a wizard. In the meantime, the guards would probably mill around in confusion, or act as if the fort were under attack (they might arm the battlements and not pursue the fugitives beyond the walls of the fort).

The slow decision-making process of a committee within a bureaucracy can be simulated by casting 1d6 for each decision-maker. The total equals the number of hours, days, weeks, or months required for the organization to reach a consensus. Decide which unit of time to use based upon the urgency of the issue at hand. For example, if the six members of the Fallorian Alliance must decide whether to back Bakshra's military plans against the Church of Gonroll, you might roll 6d6 and determine that they will reach a consensus in 20 weeks. However, if Bakshra begins the campaign on his own, it may take only 20 hours for the group to reach a consensus. A single reaction roll can be used to determine the ultimate decision.

This section describes how to introduce and integrate villains into your campaign. We will begin by looking at the most common ways to create a plot for your adventure. We then provide some practical advice on how to incorporate a villain into both linear and matrix adventures. Finally, we present a new way to prepare villain encounters.

Creating a Plot

Now that you have defined your villain, he is ready to enter the world of the living. Do not develop the details of your plot before the villain is created. As you will see, well-defined villains generate plots of their own. A plot reflects the unique outlook and attitudes of your villain. Your villain's actions extend logically from his motives and needs, which in turn extend from his personality and situation.

There are as many ways to create a plot as there are DMs creating them. Each method has its own advantages. The most common approaches are map first, plot first, outcome first, and villain first.

Map-First Method

Many DMs plan their adventures by creating a dungeon, then worry about how to get the player characters to go inside it (and why some villain would bother to live there in the first place). These adventures often focus on the deviousness of traps and monster encounters which each DM places in the adventurers' path.

Map-first adventures are often based upon puzzle-solving and tests of players' wits, as well as their knowledge of obscure rules. They make terrific one-shot adventures and can have a great "beer and pretzels" feel. Map-first adventures are usually linear and can accommodate, but do not require, in-depth role-playing. This makes them great for tournaments or as introductions to the game for beginners. This approach characterizes what is often called the "classic dungeon crawl."

A villain in a map-first adventure is usually an intrinsic part of the mapped area. The assumption is that some malign intelligence has laid the obstacles in the adventurers' path and may even be monitoring their progress through the complex. Villains in a map-first adventure often taunt and goad the party into moving deeper into their lairs.

Plot-First Method

After working through the map first method, many DMs build plot driven adventures. The DM develops a plot, and creates the necessary characters and settings to lure the player characters into the action. This approach is often used when creating mysteries.

In plot-first adventures, the action drives the characters. For example, a DM may decide that the crown jewels will be stolen and the PCs hired to uncover the thief. The DM has probably devised a crafty way for the villain to have stolen the jewels, such as a *passwall* spell used by a sneaky wizard, and created clues for the players to piece together.

This approach is likely to provide more realism compared to map-first adventures. Like the map-first approach, the adventure can exist as a freestanding module independent of the wants, needs, ambitions, and desires of the characters. The problem with this approach is that the PCs are not involved in the action because of personal motivations, making a potentially less engaging scenario. Consequently, the villain might ultimately be a bad "made-for-TV-movie" throwaway without much depth.

Outcome-First Method

Some DMs create an exciting climactic or dramatic moment, working backward to create a storyline and series of events to bring that moment alive. This approach can result in memorable sessions which players will talk about for years to come: "Remember that night we finally caught up with the one-legged man and he turned out to be my character's father who had gone insane?"

The danger of this approach is that you risk compromising the players' sense of free will. The hallmark of a good DM is the ability to have your players convinced that their decisions drive the story. Players grow frustrated with a DM whose personal agenda shows through the thin veil of believability:

DM: You hear a rumor that there is a really mean dragon capturing children just west of town. You also hear that the dragon guards a ton of treasure.

PLAYER: Yeah, well, we head the other direction. East.

DM: Er, um. There's a big river east of town that looks too wide to cross.

PLAYER: We buy a boat.

DM: There aren't any boats in town. In fact, the town's boat-builder has been killed.

PLAYER: I have boat-building proficiency.

DM: Well, all the trees have been burned to the ground by the dragon, and there's a giant whirlpool in the river which the townspeople say has never been passed.

PLAYER: OK, OK. We head north.

DM: There's an impassable mountain range to the north.

PLAYER: South.

DM: Uh, OK, um, you head south and an endless desert stretches out before you.

PLAYER: All right, already! We'll go fight your stupid dragon.

Villain-First Method

Using this approach, you create a complete villain before deciding on his actions. A complete villain creates plots of his own. As he grows and changes, experiencing successes and defeats, he will do the work for you. You can still incorporate all the fun of an exciting dungeon, a devilish conspiracy, or a dramatic moment, which all extend logically from the villain in control.

Focusing on characterization brings believability and internal consistency to your adventures. You will begin to ask yourself what sort of person lives on the tenth level of an underground dungeon—clearly, someone who is somewhat impractical, extremely paranoid, and incredibly wealthy (with knowledge of engineering). You may also begin to ask yourself questions like, "How *exactly* does your dungeon-dwelling villain manage to conduct his affairs with all those wandering monsters scooting around his place?"

The risk of creating a villain-first adventure is that the villain may not logically end up in the players' path. It is sometimes best to start with the kernel of a plot idea, develop your villain based upon this, then allow him freedom to pursue other acts of villainy if he survives the initial adventure.

Essential Components of Your Plot

Plot is action. It is the process of overcoming obstacles to achieve a goal.

Actions emerge from the needs of villains. In turn, these actions have an impact upon your player characters. The villain does not necessarily need to initiate the process. In fact, the actions of your PCs may provoke a response from a dormant villain. There are only two components essential to the plot in role-playing games. First, something of great importance to either your villain or heroes should depend upon the actions of the other. Second, these events should arise logically.

For example, it is not enough for Bakshra to stop the flow of snappy hats into the heroes' town. Your player characters are unlikely to care about the availability of headwear, and it is even more unlikely that Bakshra would have an interest in preventing people from having hats. This is not to say that it is impossible, just unlikely. Based upon what we know of Bakshra, it is more likely that he would try to expand his territory into the player characters' free farmland and wipe out the clerics residing there.

Linear vs. Matrix Adventures

As we mentioned, plot is action. Now you must decide how to bring this action to life. Will you completely plan out the action ahead of time? Will you simply set up a situation and allow your players to instigate the action?

Two basic approaches can be used to prepare an adventure. Each method has many variations, and it is possible to move from one style to the other within the same campaign.

The Linear Adventure

This is the most common form of adventure. In its purest form, the linear adventure can amount to a simple dungeon crawl, with the villain waiting in the last room of the dungeon sitting on a pile of treasure. Each room has one entrance, one exit, and a monster waiting on the other side of the door. Another good example of a linear adventure is the "pick-a-path" style book, in which a reader follows the story to a point where he must select between one of several options. Each option directs the reader to continue reading at a different page.

A linear adventure can usually be drawn as a flow chart, with options and consequences represented as paths on the chart. It usually involves a series of planned encounters and fixed obstacles, which must be overcome in a certain order. The characters' actions determine what options remain available to them, as well as the likelihood of attaining their goal.

A linear adventure is usually time independent, which means that a certain event is "programmed" to take place, such as when the adventurers walk into a particular room of a dungeon. The event occurs whether the PCs walk into the room now or in 10 weeks.

The successful end of a linear adventure often involves a particular person, place, or thing which must be found, defeated, or rescued. The DM can limit the players' decisions to those bringing their characters closer to their goal.

Building a Linear Adventure

Linear adventures have a distinct advantage over other adventures: You can prepare for anything during the scenario. Even minor encounters can be planned in advance. A simple linear adventure might involve Bakshra's decision to kidnap a local cleric. A diagram of this adventure is provided on the chart on the following page.

The party is attacked by highwaymen and stands a chance of finding some treasure if it travels by land. If the group travels by sea, it is attacked by pirates and also stands to gain treasure. You could use the same treasure for either encounter. You might use the treasure as an opportunity to provide a critical clue to the adventure. On the other hand, you might want the outcome of the two encounters to be entirely different and take the party down drastically different paths toward the conclusion of the adventure.

Villains in the Linear Adventure

A linear adventure allows you to carefully plan every encounter with the villain. The risk of the linear adventure is that the villain is essentially static or one-dimensional; the villain often serves the plot in a linear adventure, rather than the plot serving the villain. Consequently, the personalities of the characters rarely change the probable outcome of the encounter. The adventure resembles an arcade video game in which players simply negotiate their way through a series of obstacles, and those obstacles behave in a predictable and programmed manner.

The Matrix Adventure

Matrix adventures are designed to give the PCs greater flexibility and a wider choice of options in any given situation. A matrix also brings added realism to an adventure.

The three basic types of matrices are the space matrix, the time matrix, and the power matrix. Three types of matrices can expand the possibilities of your game: Although each has its own advantages, they also create unique problems for the DM.

The Space Matrix

A space-matrix adventure allows the PCs to explore all regions of a larger area in any order desired. For example, an adventure in an amusement park would be a space matrix. Unlike the linear dungeon in which each room has one entrance, one exit, and must be traversed in sequence, the amusement park has a variety of rides and attractions which might be visited by the adventurers at any time. In fact, the group might visit a site more than once, skipping others altogether. A pure space

THE FLOW OF A LINEAR ADVENTURE

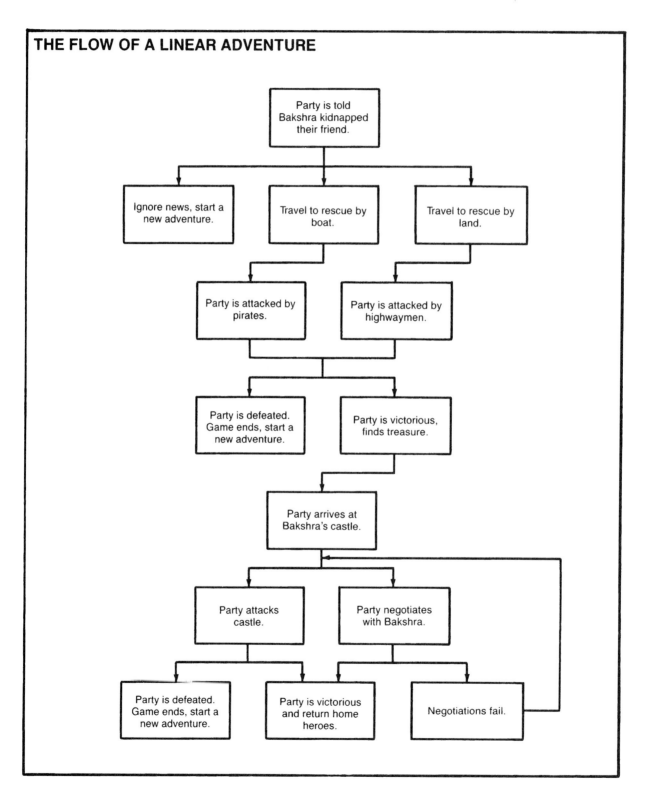

Party is told Bakshra kidnapped their friend.

- Ignore news, start a new adventure.
- Travel to rescue by boat.
- Travel to rescue by land.

Party is attacked by pirates.

Party is attacked by highwaymen.

Party is defeated. Game ends, start a new adventure.

Party is victorious, finds treasure.

Party arrives at Bakshra's castle.

Party attacks castle.

Party negotiates with Bakshra.

Party is defeated. Game ends, start a new adventure.

Party is victorious and return home heroes.

Negotiations fail.

matrix places no linear constraints on the outcome of the adventure. It might involve a quest to collect a list of spell components from several wizards in different villages, each of which can be visited in any order without affecting the likelihood of success.

The advantage of a space matrix is the flexibility it affords the PCs. Players enjoy having freedom of will without feeling corralled down a particular path. The weakness of this type of matrix is the difficulty it presents the DM in controlling the action. No encounter depends upon the outcome of any previous encounter. A purely spatial matrix ends up feeling more like a trip to a shopping mall rather than an epic adventure; it is difficult to build intensity or momentum unless some linear elements are incorporated.

Linear components can be mixed into a space matrix by making access to one physical area dependent upon previous visits to others. For example, the adventurers sent to fill a list of magic components might discover that a wizard refuses to see them until they can prove they have gathered the other components.

The Time Matrix

A time matrix is a feature which can be overlaid on your space matrix. A time matrix creates an adventure where events do not wait for player-character participation. An example of a time-matrix adventure would be a plot to assassinate a queen during her visit to a neighboring city. The city might have a number of buildings in which the queen will spend time over a period of three days. Her trip could culminate in a parade planned to run the length of the city's main street. The assassins are prepared to attack at the various buildings during the queen's visit, and are also ready to strike during the parade. In this example, you would have not only a map of the city, but notes regarding who would be where and at what times. If the PCs are not in the right place on the right day at the right time, the queen may die.

The advantage of a time matrix is that it can add momentum and drama to an adventure. When players realize that the world is not waiting for them to make decisions, they soon develop a sense of urgency regarding how they use their time. The disadvantage of a time matrix is that it can be very unforgiving of player-character mistakes. It is sometimes best to use time as a way of changing the direction of an adventure, rather than making the ultimate success of the adventure dependent on a particular hour or date. Instead of making a queen's life dependent upon the PCs' timing, allow time to tilt the balance of power in the adventure. For example, in a war between two kingdoms, time may influence which neutral parties ally with the heroes; time does not need to determine the outcome of the war.

The Power Matrix

A power matrix is a radically different approach to adventure design, and it can be incorporated into a game already using a space and time matrix. It should only be used if you prefer improvisation to planned encounters. In a power matrix, you do not plan a sequence of events or the ultimate outcome of an adventure. You simply design a set of relationships between a variety of NPCs and plan one encounter to serve as a hook for the adventure. Once the story has started, you allow the diverse needs and personalities of all the characters involved to perpetuate the plot.

Don't use the power matrix if you do not like the possibility of significant and unpredictable power shifts in your campaign. In addition, a power-matrix adventure is more likely to split

a party, or wind up with a lack of focus, than a well-planned linear adventure.

One method of building a power-matrix adventure is to create two or more diverse individuals or groups with mutually exclusive goals. Prior to the entrance of the player characters, neither party is in a position to significantly advance its own interests. The heroes may have incentive to ally with any of the parties, but cannot ally with all of them. They may also have incentive to act independently. In a sense, you are trying to create a state of equilibrium which the PCs shift, before you restore a new (and different) state of balance. You do not plan an adventure, you simply design the relationships. The characters and their interactions with various parties create the adventure. The key to creating relationships allowing improvisation is to design ties between the parties, making certain that everyone wants something from someone else. This creates a web of power relationships.

For example, if Pandar is dependent upon Bakshra for his job, this gives Bakshra power over Pandar. If Pandar can find no other source of employment, this increases the power which Bakshra has in the relationship. If Pandar can easily find a job in the next town, this lessens Pandar's dependency upon Bakshra, and in turn lessens Bakshra power in the relationship. The more places Pandar can find work, the less dependent he is on Bakshra. If Pandar is the only one who can do his job, this gives him power over Bakshra. If no one could be found and trained to do Pandar's job, this would increase Pandar's relative power in his relationship with Bakshra.

By introducing more parties into a situation and creating a matrix of dependency, you create a stockpile of ready adventures. A simple example of this type of stockpile is the classic range war, where the farmers need the land for raising crops, and the cattlemen need the land for their herds. A merchant may purchase goods from both the farmers and the cattlemen depending on the changing market. The town marshal may have an interest only in preserving the peace.

To get the story rolling, the DM may not even need to provide a hook. Treating the town as a space matrix, the PCs can wander into the adventure from any direction. Depending on where they decide to stop, they are likely to encounter one of the parties in the conflict, and may wind up forming an alliance simply because of who they found first.

You might also choose to hook the party with a planned encounter. The PCs could witness a murder associated with the conflict, and the town marshal insists they remain until the issue is resolved. Once the action begins, you will find that the diverse needs and goals of your NPCs keep the story moving.

The strength of this type of adventure is that the DM serves as an impartial moderator with no vested interest in the adventurers' course of action. Instead, the DM focuses on the *consequences* of the adventurers' decisions; he doesn't force the action in a particular direction, giving ultimate freedom to the players. Also, a power-matrix adventure forces the DM to develop areas of his campaign world which might otherwise be neglected.

These adventures have another interesting attribute: The identity of the bad guys is not always clear. The villains may emerge only as the conflict evolves, and villainous character traits are usually defined through the conflict. It may turn out that there are villains nesting on all sides of a conflict.

The difficulty of running a power matrix is that you cannot plan the adventure in great depth because the actions of the NPCs are, in part, a reaction to the environment. However, you *can* plan the next scenario if you get some indication of the players' intentions.

A SPACE MATRIX ADVENTURES

The Mission:
Collect a magic component from a wizard in each of the eight villages and return with them to the castle so that the king may be cured.

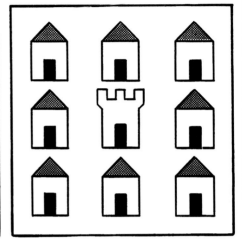

A SPACE/TIME MATRIX ADVENTURE

The Mission:
Collect a magic component from a wizard in each of the villages and return with them to the castle so that the king may be cured.

The wizards frequently visit one another. For any village visited, roll 1d6. The wizard is out on a 1 or a 2. The wizard is in on a 3 or 4. The wizard is being visited by another wizard on a roll of 5 or 6. Use 1d8 to determine which wizard is visiting.

It takes one day to travel between adjacent villages. It takes one day to travel from the castle to any village. You have 12 days to complete the mission.

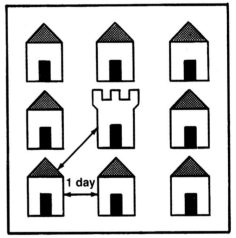

A POWER MATRIX ADVENTURE

The Mission:
Collect a magic component from a wizard in each of the eight villages and return with them to the castle so that the king may be cured.

In addition to the rules established in the Space/Time Matrix Adventure, you are to consider the following rumors:
1. One of the wizards is actually trying to kill the king.
2. One of the wizards wants to fake the king's death in order to expose the king's enemies.
3. One of the wizards will ally with the highest bidder.
4. One of the wizards wants to become counselor to the king.

You do not know to which wizard any of these rumors may apply.

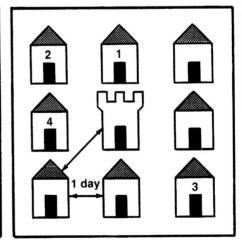

Villains in a Matrix Adventure

Matrix adventures lend themselves to complex political intrigue. With a power matrix, alliances can shift and treachery may lie in the heart of your closest ally. It is important to allow a distinct villain to emerge from the shadows early in the adventure, serving as a focus for the player characters' actions. Once they have a direction, you may orchestrate shifts in the relationships and the appearance of new villains, allies, and traitors.

It is also possible to create a muddle of intentions; the PCs are never certain who to trust or who to oppose. Players may have difficulty with too much ambiguity. If you interpret an event in two ways, a group of six players will come up with six different interpretations and overlook the two you thought obvious. When running a matrix adventure, the most important job for the DM is to know when to provide direction to the players. This prevents them from growing frustrated, or moving in circles. The players will usually have less difficulty if a distinct villain emerges quickly.

A Third Option

When deciding whether to create a linear or matrix adventure (or some combination of the two), the best approach is the one which you and your players enjoy most. If you have limited time, or want to prepare in advance, it is best to lean toward a linear adventure.

If you have more planning time and are trying to develop an ongoing campaign world, matrix adventures can force you to develop aspects of your world which might otherwise be ignored. While a detailed matrix might require more initial preparation, you can often improvise a significant amount of the action by understanding your NPCs' goals and desires.

The third option is a combination of linear and matrix adventures that maintains the "feel" of a matrix. The primary attraction of the matrix is that players believe they are in control of their characters' actions and have a multitude of options at every step. With a well-thought-out combination of linear and matrix tactics, you can create a hybrid adventure that maintains the illusion of complete freedom of action while there are actually only a few likely outcomes in any encounter.

Enter the Villain

Now that your villain has a plot in motion, you need to know how he reacts when he meets your player characters. Your primary guide is the villain's personality. The villain's actions must be consistent with his character. The illusion of reality requires consistency and attention to detail. The villain needs to react consistently. You do not want a greedy villain who one day happily accepts a bribe but is indignant when offered another. In this section, we will step through a series of questions you should answer before running an encounter that involves your villain. You will see that with a well-defined character in a focused moment, random rolls on reaction dice are unnecessary.

For example, the player characters travelled unwittingly through Bakshra's territory and were attacked by his knights, the Bloodhounds. The attack seemed to single out the cleric in the party, but it left the group badly injured.

The PCs decide to seek shelter in a keep which stands on a hill overlooking the territory. It is Bakshra's keep. You decide that they will meet the lord of the manor on his way home from a hunt.

What Are the Villain's Circumstances?

He is just returning from a recreational hunt, where he released a cleric in the woods to be hunted by his men and dogs. He is surrounded by a hunting party of six knights and a pack of hounds. He is exhilarated.

What Just Happened to the Villain?

He successfully ended the hunt himself by running the cleric to exhaustion and killing him with his scourge. He is riding home joking with his men.

What Is the Villain's Ultimate Objective?

Eliminate the cloudy lies of religion by destroying all churches.

What Is His Current Objective?

To find out who is in the band of armed strangers approaching his keep. He thinks they may be emissaries from one of his allies. He would also like to get home before nightfall.

How Will He Achieve This Objective?

He will send out one of his men ahead of the pack to identify the party of adventurers, and interrogate them himself, if necessary.

What Will This Character Do?

If you are uncertain how to respond, remember that in a crisis, a person often relies on well-developed abilities. For example:

Let's assume the party takes a defensive posture toward the approaching rider, and requests aid for their dying cleric friend. From what we know of Bakshra, he is not a man given to sud-

den deception. It may occur to him to invite the party to his castle in order to nurse the cleric back to health, then release him in a hunt. However, it is likely that his first thought will be to finish the cleric off. Given his state of mind following the hunt, and given the fact that he is likely to be suspicious of the visitors, he may simply state, "You are welcome to stay at my home, but I'm afraid there is nothing that can be done to help your friend. Best just to end his suffering," upon which he might bring his horseman's mace down upon the wounded cleric.

If you consider these questions before any encounter in which your villain confronts the player characters, you will find it much easier to make decisions on the villain's behalf. If you are creating a linear adventure, you should take a moment to jot down your thoughts on each question. If you are improvising, you should still take a moment before the villain makes an entrance to ensure that his actions are consistent with his character.

In this chapter, you will learn how to individualize your villain and heighten the believability of the game's drama. This can be done through role-playing the villain and creatively describing events to your players.

Role-Playing Your Villain

It is usually more dramatic for your players to learn about a villain through your role-playing rather than by describing the villain's personality. You have a number of vehicles to help characterize your villain.

Facial Expression

Your villain's facial expression contributes significantly to engaging your players' interest. Does your villain have a habitual expression? A unique expression helps your players recognize the villain in recurring encounters. If you suddenly assume the familiar squint of an old enemy when the player characters enter a room, it may be more effective than announcing, "You open the door to find your old arch-rival Saucy Jack squinting in his characteristically shifty manner." How does your villain use his eyes and his glance? At whom does he look when speaking? A villain may not necessarily use his face to show his emotions or mood.

Depending on his personality, the villain may be more or less inclined to allow his face to indicate his emotions in different situations. For example, people avoid allowing superiors to see indications of anger, disappointment, or other negative emotions.

Voice

Varying your manner of speaking is the most common method used by DMs to individual-ize their NPCs. Tone of voice, modulation, tempo, and choice of words all contribute to bringing your villains to life. Unfortunately, DMs fall into ruts in how they use their voices. Don't alter your natural manner of speaking unless you can individualize the character, otherwise every innkeeper begins to sound the same. Altering one aspect of speaking can often conjure a minor character for the moment.

Choice of words can also characterize a villain. Don't we speak differently when we are at home than when we appear in a court of law? Wouldn't a professor of entomology speak differently than a gas-station attendant who collects bugs in his free time? A villain's vocabulary varies by his location, his knowledge, and his audience.

Gesture

Comedians mimic the habitual gestures of famous people when doing impersonations. When using gestures to characterize a villain, your approach should extend beyond "talking with your hands." Think of several ways in which someone might habitually use their hands and arms to communicate. Captain Queeg of *The Caine Mutiny* made a practice of clicking two steel balls together with one hand. One of your villains may simply rest a few fingers on his temple when speaking, as if intensely concentrating.

Habitual Posture

Posture can convey personality and emotion as effectively as voice and gesture. In cartoons, we have seen Canadian mounties stride about with their chests thrust forward and their chins held high to display bravery and self-confidence. Their adversaries skulk about with their shoulders hunched over and

hands retracted like claws to reveal a sneaky, predatory nature. A DM can communicate a great deal about a character through posture, even while sitting in a chair.

Walk

A character's walk is rarely used by DMs role-playing villains, primarily because few DMs bother to get out of their seats when moderating. It can heighten the drama of a situation considerably if you are willing to move from your chair. Use the room in which you are playing; you might circle your players, resting your hands on their shoulders, leaning between them and whispering softly. As another character, you might move to the corner of a room and turn shyly. This method should only be used to accentuate an important moment, and not mistakenly turn your

game into a live-action role-playing game.

If you make effective use of the tools available to you, the players will know when they are in the presence of their characters' adversary.

Describing Events

In addition to the times when you play the role of the villain, the manner in which you describe events can dramatically impact the game. Remember to show, rather than tell, and creatively detail the villain's depravity.

Show, Don't Tell

Whenever possible, it is always more effective for the player characters to learn about the villain's character through the villain's actions. It is much less dramatic to be told, "Bakshra is a

really mean man," than to stumble upon a family that has been attacked by his men and left to die by the roadside. However, this is not to say that unnecessary gore or gruesomeness is the key to portraying a villain.

Attention to Detail

Another tool that makes your villains more vivid is your attention to detail. You should always individualize your villain and make him distinct. The more specific the details, the more vivid the role-playing experience. Whether you are describing combat or the signing of a treaty, specificity heightens both the realism and the emotional response of your players.

If you are having trouble increasing the level of detail, take an inventory of the scene in your mind. Rather than tell the heroes that they see a small farm that looks like it was destroyed by a dragon, consider each of your senses and see if you can account for each thing they detect.

It is an overcast day. As you walk along the dirt road, you catch a faint smell of smoke carried on the wind. You crest a hill and see the ruins of a small stone house blackened from fire. A light patter of rain has started, and you can't tell if the clouds welling up from the house are smoke or steam. The rain feels cold. The blackened beams of the barn have fallen inward and collapsed on themselves.

As you walk near the house, you can see two large black patches of burned grass, what look like the smoking remains of dairy cows. You smell roasted meat.

You don't need to get carried away with it, but detail also helps to focus players' atten-

tion when they are bored or distracted. Sometimes it helps to write "read to the players" notes for planned encounters prior to a session. That way you don't have to worry about improvising prose while trying to manage combat and dice rolls.

The strange, veiled woman sat before us at her desk. She wore an exotic silk turban and a veil of linked silver coins. We had been caught stealing from her gallery of rare art objects. Her guards had dragged us before her and left. Her thin silk caftan revealed a full and curvaceous figure. My partner, Allain, gawked at her.

"So, you would steal from me?" she purred.

"No ma'am," Allain began. "We were lost. We were trying to find the proprietor to inquire about purchasing some art."

"Did you like what you saw?" she teased him. It was clear she knew exactly what we were doing. She also knew that Allain was having difficulty focusing on the conversation. He was clearly overcome by the woman's allure.

"Do you like what you see now, my thief?" she continued, dropping the coin veil from her face. Allain stepped forward to stare, blocking my view, but I knew well enough to look away when my friend suddenly turned chalky gray. I closed my eyes and buried my face in my hands as I heard the hiss of an angry nest of serpents.

The woman was a medusa.

I heard a sharp crack, then the thud of breaking stone before the woman spoke: "I will let you go, but I will keep your friend as a part of my statuary. Bring me a thousand gold pieces and he is yours. I cannot promise that I will not have sold him before you return, though damaged merchandise does not move too quickly. I have broken off his hand as a memento to remember him."

The monster threw the stone hand at my feet. My blood ran cold.

In this section, we will explain how you can turn your favorite monster into a villain. We will discuss certain traits in the monstrous race you select that are likely to make a more dramatic villain. You will learn how to create an entirely new campaign world based upon your new creations.

Villains vs. Monsters

Throughout this book, we have been talking about villains, but have not specifically explained the difference between a villain and a mere monster, or how a monster can rise to the stature of a true villain. The *DUNGEON MASTER® Guide* defines a monster as any creature that is not of a player-character race. The primary difference between monster races and player-character races is that monsters usually have a strong racial predisposition to a particular alignment. As a result, certain monsters are literally born to be bad.

How to Do It

The process of turning a MONSTROUS COMPENDIUM® entry into a villain can be even easier than creating a villain from a player-character race. The results can be perverse. You begin by reading through the entry, then follow the same process described in the first chapter of this book, "Defining Your Villain." You may be surprised by the ideas which the MONSTROUS COMPENDIUM entry provides as you develop your villain.

Three general approaches can be used to turn a monster into a villain.

Use the Entry

With this method, you create the villain within the constraints of the MONSTROUS

COMPENDIUM® entry. Some monsters, including liches, vampires, kenku, and yuan-ti, can be taken straight from the book and developed into compelling villains by using the steps for character creation. We will use this approach later to create the example of Lady Silith, a medusa.

Modify the Entry

If you think a standard monster might be interesting if it had a higher intelligence or an unfortunate shift in alignment, give it a try. An orc or troll leader might be smarter than the rest. A centaur might make an interesting foe if something had twisted its good nature toward evil. A gnoll who never breaks his word could be an interesting lawful evil variation from the "standard" chaotic evil race. Even an ordinary kobold might become more ambitious with a few more hit dice and a troll-like ability to regenerate hit points.

Freely Interpret the Original

This approach begins by simply using a MONSTROUS COMPENDIUM entry as a creative springboard. This method can be used to create a unique villain, but some players will feel cheated if every tough monster they encounter has additional powers. However, this strategy can result in dramatic ideas which may be the basis of an entire campaign. The DRAGONLANCE® and RAVENLOFT® campaign worlds are the result of this approach.

What if you created a new type of monster loosely based upon the manticore? Imagine this creature as a lawful evil beast given to organization and military enterprises. They are extremely intelligent, territorial, and hostile toward men. Suppose these creatures have destroyed the cities of man with armies of sylvan creatures, such as sprites, satyrs, dryads, and korreds, and additionally have allowed forest growth to run rampant. This is a world where man only has a few scattered villages. You could base an entire campaign on the efforts of these last outposts of humanity to organize and defend themselves from the forest folk.

Selecting a Monster

The first thing you need to do before creating your monstrous villain is select a monster to transform. Each of the MONSTROUS COMPENDIUM entries bristles with potential enemies.

Intelligence

Your new villain should be a monster of at least average (8–10) intelligence or higher, presenting an ongoing challenge to your player characters. A highly intelligent monster can anticipate the actions of the adventurers and concoct fiendish conspiracies.

Society

Monsters with some sort of society make a good foundation for a villain. A monstrous society can provide a villain with resources and assistance. It can also suggest logical objectives for your villain. Yuan-ti, kenku, and drow all have unique societies that could supply soldiers, gold, followers, or magic.

Alignment and Free Will

Most monstrous races have a particular alignment. As we will explain in the section on alignments, you should select an adversary who is evil, or has an alignment in direct

opposition to your adventurers. Evil monsters make good villains because they are less likely to compromise with their opponents.

Races who represent a variety of alignments have the added interest of being creatures who are not "born to be bad." An orc is not going to fool anyone into trusting it, and no one will be surprised when it attacks a group of helpless pilgrims. A monstrous villain is more despicable if it has a wide range of moral and ethical options but has chosen a path of corruption.

Monster Problems

Regardless of the approach you use to turn your monster into a villain, feel free to play with the motives and objectives of the monster. Any monster rising to villain status is a unique and exceptional case.

You might be puzzled by a MONSTROUS COMPENDIUM® entry and wonder what plots a monster might undertake. If you don't already have a goal in mind, select a motive from the list provided in the first chapter and see what objectives might arise if that motive was excessive or twisted.

Another solution to the objective problem is to develop a creature with inscrutable motives. The nice thing about summoning your villains from other planes is that they are not necessarily motivated by the same needs driving villains from the prime material plane. For example, a creature from the Elemental Plane of Water might want to collect water from human bodies in the Prime Material Plane to accomplish some goal at home. The difficulty with this approach is that you must understand your villain to avoid difficulties while role-playing.

In the following example, we will take a medusa and give her the unlikely need for affiliation with others. We will then make this need so twisted and obsessive it takes the form of finding friends and turning them to stone so she will have them forever. We will use the statistics for a medusa straight from the MONSTROUS COMPENDIUM, though her character is unique for her kind.

Lady Silith, a Medusa

Occupation

Lady Silith is an art dealer. Her enormous caravan of extraordinary artworks is legendary. She is believed to trade with the duergar dwarves living in neighboring mountains. The remarkable sculptures which she has supposedly obtained from them have been purchased by aristocrats and nobles throughout the region. She is not publicly known to be a medusa.

Objective

According to the AD&D® MONSTROUS COMPENDIUM entry, medusas are sometimes driven to mate with humanoid males. The act always ends in the male's death, usually by petrification, when the medusa reveals her previously hidden face.

Silith is ultimately searching for a mate to begin her brood.

Motive

Medusas are normally hateful and isolated creatures. However, Silith is overwhelmed by a need for affiliation, explaining her fascination with human company.

Personality

Dominant Trait 1: Vindictive
Dominant Trait 2: Deceitful
Contradictory Trait: Aesthetic

Since her emergence into human society, Silith has taken pleasure in the suffering of others. She

particularly delights in destroying those she believes have brought her harm or offense.

Silith is a cunning and deceitful creature. She always fulfills her business contracts to the letter, but not to the spirit of their intent. Curiously, the medusa has astonishingly delicate sensibilities and good aesthetic taste. Even in combat, Silith waits for the "perfect moment" before turning a victim to stone, creating a sculpture that embodies a weakness of that particular species or being.

Attitudes and Behaviors

Silith holds humanity in contempt; she considers them a morass of hypocritical worms. However, she is intrigued by the sensitivity of the artwork which humans occasionally create. She plays the coy and doting patron to artists, actors, and bards.

Silith generally treats people with transparent gentility. Her honeyed words have a caustic edge and belie an imperious manner.

Tastes and Preferences

Silith collects carpets, paintings, and sculpture. She has an excessive interest in the human body, and enjoys attending formal dances where she can sit and watch bodies in motion. She also enjoys seeing unusual creatures, and has collected a small menagerie of strange monsters in her caravan. She pays dearly for art objects, people, or creatures that capture her interest.

Surroundings

Silith spends most of the year traveling from the court of one noble house to another. Her caravan train consists of several large wagons loaded with the stone remains of her victims, which she sells at her stops. Several more wagons are loaded with paintings, rugs, and art objects. She travels with 20 soldiers and a blind manservant.

Silith is rumored to have a supply house in the mountains attended by duergar slaves. It is believed that her true home is the lavish palace of her father in the far east.

History

Silith grew up in a cavern to the east. Her mother died a natural death when Silith was very young. Her loneliness became an obsessive greed for companionship. She delighted making wandering travelers and stray animals stay in her lair as guests of stone. However, she grew bored with the mountaineers, dwarves, and deer who seemed to be the only creatures to stumble into her home.

One day, a party of adventuring thieves found her cave. They planned to hide out for a few days after having robbed a caravan of valuable artwork. Silith allowed the group to wander through the halls and tunnels of her lair. She followed them, waiting for a moment to reveal herself to each. As the party dwindled, the group's panic increased. Finally, the last survivor collapsed to the ground and broke into hysterical tears.

Silith was intrigued by the man's behavior. In broken sobs, the thief recounted all the things he would never see again. Silith listened as the thief described vivid memories of gold sculptures, green fields, and merry parties.

Silith finally spoke. She told the broken man she would spare his life if he would show her the wonders of his stories. The astonished thief readily agreed. Silith emerged from the shadows behind the prone man and told him that while he would live, he would never see the world of which he spoke. She plunged her fingers into the thief's eyes. Several days later, with a portion of the stolen treasure and a veil, Silith and the thief emerged from the mountain, beginning her life among men.

The majority of Silith's time is spent collecting artwork and unusual animals, which she takes back to her lair and turns to stone. She

delights in poetry and music, and seduces talented men and women to visit her lair, eventually adding them to her collection. Silith also enjoys large parties; they remind her of the enormous main hall of her home where the statues number in the hundreds and look like participants at a ghastly festival.

Network

Silith is well connected at the highest levels of society, and is often invited to stay at palaces and mansions. Her wealth attracts the curious and ambitious. The mark of achievement among bards in the region is to have been invited to dinner by Lady Silith.

Appearance

The mysterious Lady Silith is rumored to be a woman of heart-stopping beauty. She is never seen in public without a large turban and a veil of silver coins forged into a scaled drape. She favors silk robes, which accentuate her curvaceous figure, and intricately embroidered cloaks. She is rumored to be the daughter of a sultan to the east, and that she remains covered because her great beauty would diminish the glory of her artwork.

The MONSTROUS COMPENDIUM® can be a nearly endless source of unique villains. By employing the villain definition tools, you will be surprised at how much depth and character you find in a familiar monster.

Monsters as Henchmen

We waited in the court of Dranthen Tower to give Bakshra a formal protest from the church of Gonroll for the harassment of the local clergy. Masley, the bishop of Borderton, accompanied us. He paced nervously as we waited.

Suddenly, Bishop Masley clutched at his throat as blood funneled through his fingers and down his tabard. The stunned priest collapsed backward. One of my men caught him under the arms and dragged him toward the castle gate. The rest of us drew our swords and surrounded the bishop to protect him from further attack.

That was the first time we ever saw the work of Scrolokk, the warlord's kenku assassin. It was not the last time we would face his bloody handiwork.

Approach the creation of monstrous henchmen and flunkies as you would ordinary henchmen, with an eye to the same issues you consider when creating monstrous villains. Look at the needs that perpetuate the relationship between the villain and the monster. Additionally, when choosing a monster for a henchman, you consider the intelligence, society, and alignment of the monster's race. Finally, you should decide whether you want to use the MONSTROUS COMPENDIUM entry straight, or modify it to suit your tastes. The four needs which you should consider in defining your monstrous henchman's relationship with the villain are reviewed below:

1. Villain's practical need
2. Villain's emotional need
3. Supporting character's practical need
4. Supporting character's emotional need

When creating monstrous henchmen, these four acquire a slightly different focus. These four needs essentially address the reason for the villain and the monster's involvement. The explanation should be consistent with the villain's personality, as well as the personality of the monster.

When creating a monstrous henchman, you may be inclined to deviate from the MONSTROUS COMPENDIUM® entry and "interpret" your own version of the species. This often occurs through your effort to logically explain the monster's association with the villain. Unless this radical race variation has been firmly established in your campaign (such as the draconian armies of the AD&D® DRAGONLANCE® world), you face two risks when using a monster interpretation. The first risk is that players become frustrated, seeing the altered creature as a device to cheat them out of glory. The second risk is that your newly created henchman steals the show from the villain. While your henchmen should be interesting, they should never be more interesting than the master villain. For example, Goldfinger's sidekick, Oddjob, used a signature weapon of a hat with a blade built into the brim, but he never diminished the reader's interest in his boss. The flying monkeys serving the Wicked Witch of the West in *The Wizard of Oz* added an element of terror, but there was never a doubt of the source of evil.

Freely interpreting a monstrous race to create a henchman can work if the newly created race has been previously established in the campaign, or is integrated as part of the adventure itself. You might create an adventure in which the villain is breeding this new monstrous variant, and the henchman serves as a testimony to the threat presented by the villain's success. The adventure might begin with the heroes following the henchman's trail of destruction, eventually facing the master villain himself. The villain might also be working to bring the newly created race from another plane into the world of the player characters.

In this section, we have focused on monsters in the role of henchmen or servants to a villain. As we established in the chapter on supporting players, the monster does not need to serve the villain as a henchman. It may be a neighbor, a business partner, a teacher, a mentor, a tenant, a supplier, or a friend.

The same creation issues face the monsters surrounding the villain, as those who serve him directly. A minor character who is not a servant of the villain is not perceived by players as a gift to the villain from the DM. For this reason, you may feel more comfortable exercising a greater degree of latitude in modifying the statistics of the monster. You only need to worry about game statistics if your player characters are going to fight these minor characters.

The following example introduces Scrolokk, the kenku assassin, a new supporting character for Bakshra.

Scrolokk

The kenku assassin who makes his home in the Bakshra's court at Dranthen Tower.

Dominant Trait 1: Cunning
Dominant Trait 2: Reserved

1. Villain's practical need: Staff Assassin
2. Villain's emotional need: Nurturance
3. Character's practical need: Revenue
4. Supporting character's emotional need: Affiliation

Bakshra found the hatchling Scrolokk on a hunt. He returned to Dranthen Tower with the young kenku and raised him within its walls. During this time, the bird was free to travel; Scrolokk would go back to the forest for months at a time, but always returned to Dranthen Tower. Scrolokk and Bakshra became friends, and the kenku eventually served the lord of Dranthen Tower as a hired thief and assassin. Scrolokk is curious but distrustful of humans other than Bakshra, and is unlikely to parlay or bargain.

This chapter describes a variety of unique villains to add variety and excitement to your game.

Recurring Villains

> We rose from the table and paid the tab. Suddenly, we heard a shriek, and the barmaid stumbled out of the back room, retching. Quickly drawing our swords, we jumped over the bar. As we stepped into the back room, a shadow swept across the doorway. Derik, the innkeeper, swung from the ceiling. The man had been killed and hung by his feet. Boris, our lockpick, fainted.
>
> We secured the tavern and sent for the constable. We sat drinking while Boris recovered.
>
> "It's been years since I've seen anything like this," Boris began. "Darkon was once a ranger who abandoned the path of good for the lure of easy money. I first ran into him when I started my trade. He led a gang of thugs who ambushed my party in the woods. I escaped, but later returned to find the whole group had been strung up like poor Derik."

Recurring villains always engage your players' interest. A primary example of this is the Batman, who seems to encounter nothing but recurring villains. While you might question his effectiveness when he can't keep his adversaries off the streets, old enemies, like old friends, make any encounter more fun.

A Good Recurring Villain

A good recurring villain provides a formidable adversary for your player characters over an extended period. This means your villain grows in power and influence at the same time as your player characters, while remaining proportionately more powerful than the characters.

A villain's rise in power can be a direct result of the adventurers' actions, or failure to act. Other times, a dramatic increase in power is a source of mystery.

> Boris continued. "The following year, the Thane of Bunder hired my new group to recover a valuable pendant that had been stolen by Darkon's gang. We trapped him in the forest, but we were forced to let him go in exchange for the safe return of the pendant. We spent the rest of the year driving a thieves' guild from Bunder. We didn't realize at the time that Darkon would organize his own men and step in to fill the void."

Providing your recurring villain with an evil organization to run, or one in which he can be a member, ensures you can provide your villain resources to conduct his plots and combat your heroes. In addition, you create a structure from which new opponents may appear when that villain is defeated.

> "The next year, the people in Bunder took ill. A man showed up with a concoction that cured the illness. Half the town spent their life savings for his 'healing potion' before the Thane hired us. Sure enough, Darkon was behind it. He had set up his own thieves' guild in Bunder and poisoned the town's water supply to raise money. It took us the rest of that year to drive him and his guild from the streets. It was tough, because he always managed to come up with more men, money, and magic.

> "We trailed Darkon for years and finally cornered him in Ragged Pass. During the fight, he lost his footing and fell into the chasm. That was three years ago. We all thought he was dead."
>
> I tried to console the shaken dwarf. "Boris," I said, "that was a long time ago, and Bunder is a long way from here. He probably *did* die back then. I'm sure this is just the work of some lowlife who worked with him."
>
> As I finished speaking, the door blew open and the constable strode in, surrounded by armed men.
>
> "Well, then. What's all this about an unhappy innkeeper?" the man bellowed.
>
> Boris gasped. "It can't be. It's him!"

In our example, a party of low-level adventurers was robbed by a brutal thief and his gang of thugs. Several adventures later, they were hired to recover an item stolen by the same thief. They let the thief escape, allowing their old nemesis to grow in power (becoming the head of a thieves' guild) until the party ran afoul of another plot. Driven out of town, the villain was believed dead, only to turn up as a constable and, as the party later discovers, captain of a neighboring king's personal guard. If the party does not destroy the villain in this adventure, the king may die under mysterious circumstances and "will" his holdings to our evil thief.

Our party has crossed and recrossed paths with Darkon during his career. It is possible that the villain's first appearance was a random encounter, and the DM slowly groomed him for bigger and badder things. Darkon's power has grown along with the party's. He has always had command of greater resources than the party. He has never seemed unbeatable, just lucky. If Darkon had been killed by the PCs, his second-in-command could have vowed revenge upon the party, introducing a new party-villain relationship.

The most important thing to keep in mind when creating a recurring villain is that he should be one you enjoy role-playing. You will spend a lot of time in this character's shoes, so make sure you are going to have some fun.

Keeping Track of Your Villains

Keep a file of all of your nonplayer characters (especially your villains) on paper or note cards. Make notes of encounter dates with your PCs. Review these cards to decide what the villains have been doing between encounters with the PCs.

Your villain's world keeps turning without the adventurers' interference. For example, the cruel sheriff they once tried to discredit formed an alliance with an enemy army to bring down the throne. The possibilities are endless, but you need to keep track of your dormant villains. A helpful tool for doing this is a *campaign calendar*.

A campaign calendar is essentially a date book by which you track the progress of your party in game time. Usually, a DM makes notes about the party's arrival at certain locations, as well as memorable events. This becomes even more important when a DM is running several groups of players in the same campaign world. It's always confusing if one group is attacked by a dragon that the other killed in an earlier game. Keeping track of your villains on a regular basis helps sustain the continuity in your game.

When drawing up your campaign calendar sheets, include a list of all of your major villains. Make a note next to each name regarding

the villain's actions at the end of the game month. Only a brief note is necessary, but you may find your villains are maintaining healthy lives of depravity that may provide the hook for your adventurers' next session. You may also want to add a monthly entry for your villainous organizations on their record sheets.

A game calendar is a useful tool to keep track of *any* of your key NPCs. You wouldn't want the bad guys to gain the upper hand because they are busy every month while everyone else sits around.

An example of the types of notes you might make are illustrated below:

Dollifer, 2nd month of the year
Bakshra: Sent a request for Fallor to come to Dranthen Tower; he is planning to seize some of the free farmland on his border.

Darkon: Is taking over more responsibilities for his king. He is also extorting money from tradesmen for protection from thieves.

Lady Silith: Is traveling to Riverrun for the annual bards' festival.

Pulmer, 3rd month of the year
Bakshra: Decided to stir up trouble with the orcs. If he makes things tough on them they will begin raiding the farmers. It won't be long before the farmers turn to him for help.

Darkon: More of the same. Murdered an innkeeper who refused to pay him off.

Lady Silith: Has arrived in Riverrun. A knavish bard plans to seduce her and run off with her money.

Haddbin, 4th month of the year
Bakshra: The Bloodhounds are patrolling the farmland at the farmers' requests. The farmers are divided about the presence of the knights.

Lady Silith: Is remaining in Riverrun, negotiating a deal for a statue to be placed in the town square. It is being noted for its remarkable resemblance to a local bard who has not been seen for awhile.

A villain with an ongoing life within your campaign world contributes to the game's richness and depth. The following are templates you can apply to better define your recurring villains.

The Rival

> Thoto stared at us from across the green, fletching his arrows. A handful of mercenaries, and one or two men from the town militia, all waited with us near the castle gate. After an hour or so, the king's messenger appeared on the wall and cried, "For crimes against the crown, a price of 100 gold pieces will be given for the half-elf Pawtooth. Dead or alive."
>
> Thoto strode toward the wall to take a copy of the decree. He did not meet our gazes as he passed. He muttered, "Eight of you? And what, no marching band? You might as well stay in town. You won't catch him, and you and your friends might get hurt out there."

The rival is a unique adversary who may not be a villain, but always adds interest to any adventure. A rival can be used to add color to a larger story, like the race between General George Patton and General Bernard Montgomery to take Sicily in the movie *Patton*. A rivalry may also become the central theme of the story if the rival's villainy overshadows all other issues, as it did in *The Duelists*. In that movie, a young soldier was sent to retrieve an officer, and inadvertently

insulted him. The officer, obsessed with honor, continually challenged the younger man to a duel, but each time the duel was delayed. The obsessive rivalry continued for years until the two had their final duel.

Competing for a Common Goal

The essence of any rivalry is competition over a particular goal. The more important the goal to the player character, the more intense the rivalry. This goal can take a wide variety of forms. One character, jealous for the respect of other patrons in a bar, may challenge the party to a drinking contest or arm wrestling match. In another instance, a rival may be exploring ruins seeking the same treasure as the player characters. The rival may simply share a passion for the same lover. In our example, Thoto is a bounty hunter who has taken the same commission as the player characters to hunt down a half-elf named Pawtooth.

A difference in style can be the basis for a rivalry, or at least contribute another dimension to a rivalry. In our example of Thoto, we see a contrast between the style of the lone bounty hunter versus the adventurers who work as a team. Other such polarities could be developed around conflicts between magic versus muscle, or stealth versus forthrightness.

Coming Back for More

Rivalries work best in a campaign when the rival is a recurring character. What if Thoto is a bounty hunter who turns up now and then, chasing the same opponent as the player characters? After having their target snatched out from under them a few times, the players may begin to build an emotional stake in besting their rival.

We had finally tracked the half-elf Pawtooth to an abandoned mine in the hills north of town. We decided to pitch camp just outside the mine entrance and set up a watch while we made our plan to capture Pawtooth.

We had just finished watering the horses when Boris, keeping guard, waved us to silence. We scrambled to the edge of the small rise where the dwarf watched the dark mine entrance.

We heard a clatter of stones from the shadows and made out a figure leading another man on a horse. It was Thoto, the body of the renegade half-elf slung over his horse. He squinted as he emerged into the daylight. A grin of recognition came over his face as he saw us. He said nothing, heading down the path toward town.

Who Said Life Was Fair?

An effective rival should be matched with the PCs so they have a chance of overcoming this adversary. Varying a rival's strength from encounter to encounter can create interesting situations for your players. Ask yourself, how will they react to a rival who has repeatedly "beaten" them when they find him vulnerable? What will their reaction be when a previously weak rival suddenly appears in a position of strength? These encounters can be exciting, particularly when the stakes are raised. The player character who lends a hand to a rival may have a different outlook when the rival stabs him.

It was hard to believe. Thoto had sneaked into the thieves' lair and reclaimed the Star of Jarette for the king before we had arrived on the scene. Now he was lying at the bottom of the pit. He

had beaten us to our quarry again, but this time grew careless in his rush. The bountyhunter's leg was badly twisted. His expression showed no trace of his pain.

"Hey, Thoto. Toss up the gem, and we'll pull you out of there," Boris called.

"I don't know what you mean," he answered.

"Well, that's too bad," Boris replied. "I guess we'll have to leave you there until the goblins come for you." When he had stopped pandering the bountyhunter, Boris gleefully allowed a marble-sized gob of spit to hang precariously over the injured man. Thoto's expression suddenly changed to disgust.

"All right! You can have the gem. Just don't let that dwarf spit on me!"

Friend, Enemy, or Both!

One of the interesting features about rivals is that their relationship with the player characters may vary dramatically. It is possible for a rival to act as an ally in one encounter, and a mortal enemy in another. Embarrassing a friendly rival in public may change the nature of the relationship. A friendly rivalry is an effective way of introducing a character who eventually reveals himself to be a truly vile villain through ensuing conflicts.

In our example with Thoto, the PCs may one day find that the bounty hunter has been hired to track them. After a long hunt, the players may be forced to kill their old foe, or he may in turn trap them but decide to set them free. Then again, something entirely different may happen.

> After we had returned victorious to the king with the Star of Jarette, Thoto had taken a commission from the thieves to bring back the party (dead or alive) that had "stolen" their gem. Fortunately for us, Thoto liked to take his quarry alive. He considered it more of a challenge, and he liked to leave a trail of living enemies. We had been walking with our hands bound for two days since we were caught.
>
> Thoto had just finished feeding us, when Boris suddenly bolted for the trees; his dwarven legs could not carry him very quickly. Thoto drew an arrow from his quiver and nocked it in one steady motion. Boris turned toward Thoto, half panting and half laughing.
>
> "Come on, Thoto!" he cried. "You wouldn't shoot a man in the—"
>
> The arrow caught Boris in the throat. The dwarf pawed at his matted beard in disbelief before pitching forward into the leaves. Thoto strode over to the body and idly emptied the dwarf's pockets. He finally turned toward us. "I thought I said you can get hurt out here."

Another Dimension to Your Story

One of the strengths of a rivalry is that it adds depth to a larger adventure. The rival and the player characters may both seek to thwart the plans of the central villain. The rival may enrich and complicate the story by aiding or sabotaging the adventurers' progress. Putting bitter enemies in a situation where they must cooperate to survive is another means of adding excitement to an otherwise ordinary tale. Remember that any given part of an adventure should not have too many "main" characters beside the player characters. A rivalry can become distracting from the main storyline if allowed to dominate the action.

While most rivals are only an occasional menace, you may also want to run an adventure where a rival travels with the party. A spoiled prince escorted with his fiancee to his wedding may find himself at odds with the adventurers when his betrothed takes a romantic interest in one of the PCs. What if years after the death of Boris, the party is called by the king to undertake an expedition led by Thoto? A long running relationship with a rival adds an entertaining dimension to any quest.

The Mythic or Symbolic Villain

> Its scales dully reflected the light of our torches, but not as brightly as the horde of gold upon which it sat or the rows of crooked teeth which filled its mouth.

The focus of this book is on the creation of multidimensional villains, but there may be a role for one-dimensional villains in your campaign. We run across countless villains throughout film, literature, and comic books who are symbols for particular evils. The dragon once represented mindless greed, a creature that hoarded gold which it could not spend. In mythology, divine beings embody ideas or concepts. Sleipnir, Odin's gray horse, had eight legs and could run across land or sea. The horse was the embodiment of the wind which blows over land and water from eight principal points. Mythical gods are characters who are essentially one dimensional, but certainly not uninteresting.

One-dimensional villains can sometimes focus the emotions of your PCs through simplicity.

Demigods and Deities

While gods make up a wide variety of potential villains, their overwhelming power makes them work better as sources of power for villains. Evil clerics make terrific villains, and their god can help to personify the evil worshipped by the cleric. It also creates the interesting possibility that the cleric can fall out of favor with his god, and in turn his source of power. No one ever said gods were loyal to their followers.

A variety of sources are available for incorporating gods into your campaign. *The Complete Priest's Handbook* explains in detail how to create new religions for gameplay. The *Legends & Lore* book describes the pantheon of gods from eleven different mythos. The *Monster Mythology* guide provides additional information on the gods of nonhuman races.

Lesser powers exist in the planes who gain a cult in the prime material world without the problem of bringing overwhelming power. Natural beings have also been known to attain the ability to grant power to followers. However, a creature does not necessarily need to grant power to develop a cult of followers. Volcanoes, stone idols, animals, golden statues, monsters, and men have all been objects of worship. You could invent a cult that worships an idea, such as the greed embodied by a dragon.

> The corpulent merchant, Fulgar, leaned forward and said, "You, my son, may have the makings of a candidate for the Children of the Wyrm. I saw the way you fought with your friends over your treasure, and then how you argued about how to divide the cost for the tavern room. Your friends call you petty, but I know better. You simply want what is yours. They call it hoarding. I call it wise. True, you can't use all of your food rations right now, but what if you need them later?"

> I turned to avoid the stink of his breath. I felt ashamed of these virtues he extolled.
>
> "I have built my empire in the service of the Wyrm. Every summer, we find a charitable soul by announcing the need for volunteers to aid the infirm. We choose the most selfless, the one most eager to deplete their personal well-being, and offer the victim to the ancient dragon of Ragged Pass mountain. In doing so, we are reminded of the fate of those who would give—they are taken!"

People

A one-dimensional villain can be a fascinating character. Miss Havisham of *Great Expectations* was an old spinster jilted on her wedding day. She spent the rest of her life wearing her wedding dress, lace veil, and satin shoes. She adopted a three-year-old girl, whom she raised to mercilessly break the hearts of men. Miss Havisham embodies bitter vengefulness and lasting spite.

Not every villain needs to have full-bodied depth. It can even be a refreshing change of pace to introduce such a simple and direct villain. In our example, the merchant may come to embody greed like the dragon he worships.

> As the merchant ate, he continued to talk: "It takes great discipline to see how every opportunity might best contribute to your holdings." He paused for a moment and scanned my plate, which I hadn't touched for several minutes. "Done with that, are you?" he asked. I nodded, and he speared my half-finished leg of lamb with his dagger.

"Let me teach you a lesson," he continued. "Give me a gold coin."

I reached into my purse and doubtfully passed him a gold piece.

"Excellent. Now take a close look at it," he said as he held the coin in front of me. "Seen enough?"

I nodded.

"Good." He pocketed the coin, then drank the dregs of my beer.

"What's your point?" I asked, angry. "Give me back my coin."

"I'll do nothing of the sort, boy. The point is, never give something for nothing. I'll keep the coin, because I certainly know better than to share my wisdom for free." He slid back from the table, "I'm afraid that's all I can teach you. The more *you* begin to take, the less there will be for me!"

With that, he rose from the table and left the inn, leaving me to pay for his meal.

Monsters

In role-playing games, most one-dimensional villains are monsters. Whether it is a succubus embodying lust or our dragon embodying greed, monsters make up the bulk of an adventurer's experience. The MONSTROUS COMPENDIUM® and your random encounter charts are rife with these sorts of creatures. These monsters are fun because there is no doubt that they are a problem waiting to be solved the PCs. Changing the context of a common monster can cast a fresh light on it, like our dragon that lies at the center of a cult of greed.

We hid in the mouth of the dragon's cave, watching the proceedings. What the merchant had told me was true, but there was more. The cultists carried an unconscious woman into the lair, and chanted as they emptied sacks of gold on the ancient lizard's heap. The dragon shifted on its mound and eyed them suspiciously. It tilted its head toward the spilling coins as if it could count them by listening. Suddenly, it reared up to its full height and bellowed: "The fat man. The fat man has cheated me!"

The cultists chattered to one another in confusion. Fulgar threw himself on the ground, his mask tumbling off.

"I swear to you, Great Master, I could no sooner cheat you than myself," the merchant sputtered.

"Of course you could, merchant," the dragon replied. "You have been an excellent student. I have been waiting for one of you to rise above the rest. I have been waiting for one of you whose greed became so great that he would risk his own life to hold one more coin. The rest of you have failed me."

The cultists scattered as the dragon drew in a deep breath. Birds fluttered in all directions as smoke and flame billowed from the mouth of the cave. We ran as the trees that ringed the entrance caught fire.

Whether a one-dimensional villain is a greater power, a man, or a monster, he can add fun to your adventures if used in moderation. Overuse of one-dimensional villains diminishes the realism of your campaign. Too many complex villains results in a confused "soap-opera" instead of exciting series of adventures.

Faceless Villains

> Though Havsakk had eluded our band for over five years, we instantly recognized his handiwork. Whenever his henchmen wiped out a tribe of elves, he always left one survivor tied by the wrists to a tall pole. The victim was meant to tell anyone who discovered the massacre the name of the man responsible. If no one came, the elf died of exposure.

Another fun variation on the traditional villain is the adversary who the heroes never actually meet. As with Sauron in *The Lord of the Rings,* or Professor Moriarity in the Sherlock Holmes stories, a mysterious and extremely powerful villain can wait like a spider at the center of a web of intrigue. The various plots and conspiracies which the villain initiates are carried out by underlings and henchmen. A faceless villain can also be a lone individual whose stealth allows him to "invisibly" commit outrageous acts of villainy. These two types of faceless villains are very different, and their use creates a distinctly different tone in an adventure.

Faceless Villain as Bureaucrat

This villain is the faceless planner behind an extensive villainous organization. In the classic television series "The Prisoner," a British Secret Service agent was kidnapped after resigning from his position, awaking to find himself in the mysterious Village. The storyline of each episode dealt with the prisoner's attempts to escape, which were always thwarted by the village's supervisor, Number Two.

Although the prisoner defeated Number Two in several episodes, a new Number Two was always brought in as a replacement. Number Two was always determined to find out why the prisoner retired from intelligence work. The prisoner always tried (unsuccessfully) to discover the identity of Number One.

In the case of this type of faceless villain, the heroes have to discover the existence of the villain through a pattern or consistency in plots perpetrated by the villain's underlings. In the case of Professor Moriarity, Holmes recognized an organizing force behind the crimes he was called to investigate. From robberies, to forgeries, to murders, Moriarity was never suspected until Holmes deduced that it was the former math professor who had become the Napoleon of crime.

If you want to implement this approach, it is easiest to string together a series of short adventures where several share the same organizing principle and point to a common source.

> "Well, they didn't loot the family's gold. They only killed that son who got in their way, and burned the storehouse and poisoned the fields."
> "Yeah, so?"
> "Doesn't that strike you as a little bit strange?" Tortle continued.
> "Who cares? We killed the gith, didn't we?" I said.
> Tortle turned to me, "You remember that little farm where the guy was raising herbs and spices, and his farm was wiped out by those gith?"
> "Yeah." I did remember.
> "Yeah, you killed them before we could question them. But what about that band of elves who were smuggling magic components to Balic?"
> "They were careless and somebody killed them!" I was getting annoyed with Tortle's persistence.

> "That templar in Balic was poisoned," he continued.
>
> "She should watch what she eats!"
>
> "Doesn't there seem to be something in common here?" he asked in that patronizing way that said even an idiot would understand his implication.
>
> "Yeah, I get it. It's all connected!" I responded, not really understanding.
>
> "That templar is responsible for keeping magic components out of Balic. Those farmer's spices could be used as material components in spells. Those elves were known to smuggle contraband into the city. What does all that tell you?"
>
> "Uh. It's obvious."
>
> "Someone is trying to control the traffic of magic components into Balic. Whoever is doing it is trying to eliminate potential competitors, while making it easier for himself to get the job done. I say we take a look at the merchant registry in Balic."

As a rule, player characters are intolerant of ambiguity; if you give them two clues, they'll misinterpret them both. If you toss in a "red herring," they'll be loathe to give it up.

Making a false trail work takes time. You might choose to leave a clue that connects everything together while leaving the villain in the background. In our DARK SUN® example, the villain uses gith to execute his dirty work. They might enjoy torturing their victims in a particular manner that would point back to the same group of gith.

Among the characters we have created, Fallor, the wizard at the center of Bakshra's Fallorian Alliance, would probably make the best faceless villainous bureaucrat. What would happen to the Alliance if Fallor suddenly manifested his own personal agenda beyond mere spell

research? The first clue to the adventurers that something was amiss might be revealed when the Bloodhounds thunder past a group of clerics without taking time to kill them. After several similar incidents, the party might suspect something big was afoot. Through the course of the ensuing campaign, the PCs might have to individually defeat the six warlords who make up the Alliance before destroying Fallor's power base; even if they foil his plan, they might never encounter the powerful wizard.

Faceless Villain as Professional

A mysterious professional is another approach to creating a faceless villain. This villain keeps his identity hidden, but may leave a mark of his handiwork, like a jewel thief who leaves a note to take credit for the crime. The professional might have an alter ego or persona which he assumes to perpetrate his crimes. The unmasking of an unknown villain can be the objective of a mystery, as in the story of the Phantom who plagued the Paris opera house.

When creating this type of villain, special care must be given to methods of escape. Beyond the villain's personality, their most unique ability is their elusiveness. Wizards are naturals for this, as are fighters or thieves with *rings of invisibility*. The character class most likely to confuse your adventurers is the psionicist specializing in *psychoportation*.

> We finally had him cornered. We were eager to unmask this fiend who had eluded us for so long and been the cause of so much terror. We split up. I waited outside the door of his room, and Tortle went outside the inn to wait beneath the window in case our friend got any ideas of leaping to the street.

> I drew my short sword and kicked the door open in one swift movement. The curtains of the open window fluttered in a light breeze. I looked around quickly to make certain I wasn't being tricked, then ran to the window and peered down to the street. Instead of a broken body on the ground, I saw Tortle, staring up at me.
>
> "You didn't see him?" he called.
>
> "There's no sign of him," I shouted.
>
> "That's because he jumped," Tortle answered. "There was a shimmering in the air outside the window and he leapt right into it."
>
> "Did you see him?" I asked excitedly.
>
> "Not well. He looked humanoid."
>
> "Great! Now we have a humanoid that jumps out windows and disappears."
>
> I heard a faint crackling noise and two footsteps behind me. Before I could turn, a knife penetrated my armor and I was pushed from behind. The last thing I remember before hitting the street was a voice whispering, "I thought I forgot something."

The faceless professional may not bother to avoid being seen, but escapes by assuming misleading guises. This can take the form of a character who literally uses disguises and illusions to alter his appearance. Alternately, a villain might engage in criminal activity while maintaining an outward appearance of public respectability. A member of a lawful religious community, secretly adhering to an evil cult, is an example of this type of villain.

A faceless professional generally has less longevity than the bureaucrat because he is "on the front lines." It is much more likely that the heroes will eventually unmask and defeat him.

Whether you choose to create a faceless villain at the center of a villainous bureaucracy, or one who acts as an elusive professional, you are sure to find that they provide fertile ground for creative adventures.

The Sympathetic Enemy

In the first chapter of this book, we said that a villain needs to be unsympathetic, a character the players love to hate. However, occasionally you might create a sympathetic enemy. These characters are enemies rather than true villains, by the very fact that the hero may extend some sympathy toward them.

A villain may gain the sympathy of the heroes in several ways. The villain may ultimately redeem himself, as discussed in the section "Redeeming a Villain." The villain may, to some extent, become a victim. Dracula was portrayed as this sort of character in Francis Ford Coppola's version of the story. As we explain in the section "Hero-Created Villains," this is only effective when the villain's crimes ultimately outweigh the crimes against him. Consequently, while there may be some element of sympathy for this tragic figure, the heroes are justified in destroying him.

It is worth taking time to address the idea of sympathy for an enemy. In films and literature, the most commonly encountered sympathetic enemies are the enemy warrior and the misunderstood monster.

The Enemy Warrior

The sympathetic or noble enemy warrior is a rival competing with the heroes for victory. Stories persist about codes of chivalry maintained by the flying aces during World War I. Scenes are still recreated in movies in which combatants meet at the front line, exchanging gifts and food for the holiday. A mythical war-

rior's code promoted a concept of men of war who had their own rules. The romantic notion was that were it not for the arbitrary twist of fate, you and your enemy may have fought side by side, rather than against one another.

An encounter with a warrior of Bakshra's Bloodhounds might go like this:

I spurred my horse toward the knight on the road. The man was one of Bakshra's Bloodhounds. He drew his horseman's mace and kicked his mount forward. He swung the weapon in circles as we cantered forward. As I leveled my sword at him, the massive steel ball swept past my face and yanked my weapon from my hand. We pulled around and faced off a second time.

I had no blade, and could only hope to knock him from his saddle. He traded his mace for a sword. I could not get my footing for the jump. He swung his sword

---

high, and I ducked against my horse's neck as the blade swept over my head.

On the third pass, I leapt from my saddle and was knocked from the air by a crushing blow from his shield. I lay gasping on the ground. He circled around as I crawled toward my sword. I did not look up, but heard the steady beat of his horse's hooves on the dust as he neared. I saw my sword lying in the sun within arm's reach. As I pulled myself toward it, his shadow fell across my blade. I looked up and found a sword leveled at my neck. The horseman withdrew his blade, touched the pommel to his forehead in salute, pulled his horse around, and galloped off.

The Misunderstood Monster

Monsters who earn our sympathy often appear in books and films. The rampaging

monster who destroyed Tokyo (because it can't find its baby), and the childlike monster of Dr. Frankenstein are two examples of misunderstood monsters. Like the enemy warriors, these beasts constitute enemies rather than villains.

Imagine that our heroes are called to track down a lion that wandered from the jungle to a city. They might feel badly for the frightened and confused beast. They might even try to capture it and return it to the forest. If the lion bit a passerby, they might again feel sympathy for the creature who is a slave to its instinct. On the other hand, if the lion turns the city into a killing ground, the group might have a different attitude. The adventurers would probably lose sympathy for the animal and attempt to destroy it.

The sympathy players extend to a misunderstood monster depends upon the severity of the monster's crimes and if the monster is perceived as a villain. If the monster inflicts damage disproportionate to the crimes against it, it ultimately loses the heroes' sympathy and "becomes" a villain.

Nature as Villain

The sandstorm had raged outside for the last six days. Even in our shelter, we had to keep our noses and mouths covered to avoid breathing the choking dust. Tonight, we would finish the last of our water. We had food enough to last us three more days.

"If the storm doesn't let up by tomorrow, we're done for," I began. "Look, Tortle, can't you cast one of those animal summoning spells and conjure us some dinner?"

Tortle was angry. "No, I'm not going to summon something and then eat it! Besides, nothing could get through that storm."

"Look, there have to be some snakes in these rocks. Can't you just call enough to make some stew?" I persisted.

From the snowstorms that trapped the settlers in the Donner wagon train as it tried to cross the Rockies, to the earthquakes, hurricanes, and volcanic eruptions that continue to plague mankind, nature is an overwhelming adversary. While natural disasters do not really constitute villains as defined, the blind indifference to human life which such forces embody creates an exciting adversary.

Nature can take a malign intelligence; the RAVENLOFT® setting is built upon this idea. It is a demi-plane where the land literally grows and feeds on evil. In fact, the land itself has the power to imbue its favorite creatures with powers that incite them to perform increasingly evil acts.

If you find this sort of idea exciting, you can develop a RAVENLOFT campaign, or you might create your own demi-plane where nature is more than an indifferent obstacle.

Public Opinion as Villain

The mob edged closer to us. We tried to back slowly away as we spoke.

"Grave robbers!" shouted one townsman.

"We're not grave robbers, sir. In fact, we just defeated a horde of zombies that have been roaming in your cemetery."

"That's my mother's brooch!" another shouted.

"Here," I said. "Take it!" I yanked it off Collin's cloak and tossed it into the crowd.

"That's not her mother's brooch!" Collin complained. "That's the treasure *I* found in the zombie's lair."

"No wonder the dead walk!" a woman shrieked. "These thieves defile our familys' graves!"

A stone flew from the crowd and hit Collin on the arm. We ran to our horses as the mob surged forward.

Angry townsfolk demand a lynching; a "witch" is burned at the stake; a crowd goes out of control at a soccer match. Thomas Jefferson warned us about the tyranny of the mob.

When the interests of a minority are unprotected, the majority can have them drawn and quartered. This is the dark side of democracy, and an interesting villain in a role-playing situation. Like nature, public opinion does not really constitute a villain as we have defined it, but it can be as savage as any storm.

When incorporating public opinion into a game, remember a few things: Rumor has more strength than reality; a person trying to clear his name often looks like he is lying; and public opinion is usually fueled by a small number of "opinion makers," but rumors often grow beyond the opinion makers' control and take on their own lives.

Reality vs. Rumor

In the court of public opinion, reality rarely gets a fair hearing. Pick up a weekly tabloid in any supermarket to see the absurdities that gain credibility.

The more absurd a rumor, the greater the force of its credibility. It is quite possible that a villain has hidden behind a veil of respectability and is seen as an upright citizen. How would any community react to a band of wanderers giving a community leader a hard time? Maybe the band is mistaken for agents of a local villain and are run out of town (or worse).

Incriminating Yourself

Another wonderful paradox about public opinion is the tendency for innocent people to be dismissed as crooks attempting a cover-up when they are merely trying to defend themselves. The more passionately a person objects to false accusations, the more conviction people gain about the truth of the accusations.

We walked into the tavern and ordered a meal. A drunk in the corner lifted his head just long enough to mutter, "You can tell your master in Dranthen Tower that you'll never run our village."

We looked at one another curiously. Patrons in the bar began to mutter to one another. A burly man who seemed more surly than the rest approached us.

"So, you work for Bakshra, do you?"

"Uh, no. We don't. We're mercenaries," Budlugg answered.

"Mercenaries for Bakshra, are you?"

"No. We were passing through town looking for work."

"Oh, sure, and I'm a magical fairy with tiny little wings."

As Budlugg started to reply, the man punched him in the nose.

Pundits Are Saying . . .

Rumor and public opinion usually have a single source, and information becomes wildly distorted after being unleashed by the source. For example, in politics, professional "spin doctors" try to cast events to reflect favorably on their candidate. In your game, you should appoint one or two opinion makers. The player characters may need to identify these people to support them, ally with them, threaten them, or destroy them.

Even if your PCs locate the centers of public opinion, an angry mob takes on a life of its own. Even a recalcitrant rumormonger may find it impossible to reverse peoples' attitudes.

The Danger of the Mob

When public opinion turns against a party of adventurers, the group faces a variety of consequences ranging from blacklisting to public execution. Adventurers can find businesses closing their doors to them. They can find gangs of vigilantes gathering to drive

them from town. They can even find concerned law enforcers jailing the party up to avoid trouble, regardless of its source.

Public opinion also has a plaguelike ability to spread. A party may finally clear its name in one town, only to find danger everywhere else. Even after clearing themselves, the party may find that nobles and politicians avoid them because of past controversy.

Rolling the Dice

To incorporate mob rule into a game, begin with an opinion maker and a neutral populace. The opinion maker's attitude (generally, either for or against the party) could initially serve as a four-point bonus or penalty to a reaction roll made by the crowd. After that, any significant event may require a new reaction from the crowd. For each ensuing die roll, an opinion maker's attitude can sway the roll by two points. Unless the subject of the opinion is another opinion maker, no other positions influence the randomness of the crowd's reaction.

This is one approach for moderating the court of public opinion. Don't use dice unless you feel particularly compelled. Remember, public opinion behaves as savagely and inhumanly as any villain.

Villains for Every Alignment

Every DM has a different understanding of alignment and the degree to which it impacts his campaign. For campaigns in which alliances are drawn along the lines of character's alignments, it may be helpful to have villains who oppose your heroes not only in their objectives, but also in their alignments. In this section, we will look at examples of potential villains from every alignment.

While it is obvious how villains arise from evil alignments, it is less clear how neutral and good characters can be cast as villains. Personal enemies can arise out of any alignment; for characters of the same alignment can sometimes find themselves in conflict. For example, two paladins may be blood enemies while serving their lawful good alignment.

Neutral Villains

The greatest confusion arises regarding characters of neutral alignment. According to the rules presented in the *Player's Handbook*, a character neutral to issues of law and chaos believes in maintaining a balance between all things and their opposites, including good and evil. Characters who espouse neutrality in relation to good and evil refrain from making moral judgments. The approaches that many players and DMs take toward neutral alignments is often different than the rules. If we look at the ethical dimension of order (law and chaos), most variations fall into one of three areas: balance seeking, disinterest, and opportunistic.

Ethical Neutrality as Balance Seeking

This view represents the idea that a person neutral to issues of order believes in a balance between the various components of the universe. This view also implies that a character acts to maintain such a balance. The difficulty that some players have with this concept is that it suggests such a character would act on behalf of evil if good was gaining supremacy, or vice versa. It is difficult to imagine a person holding this sort of view, though this might be the attitude of an arms dealer profiting from a balance of power between a good and evil empire by selling weapons to both sides.

The accommodation commonly made with this idea is to maintain that ethical neutrality is not a belief in the balance of all things, but a belief in the balance of law and chaos. This sort of person would feel rebellious in a totalitarian state, and would like rules in an anarchy.

Ethical Neutrality as Disinterest

Another accommodation commonly made is the interpretation of neutrality as a "flexible" disinterest. This concept holds that neutral people do not care about law and chaos, but tend to think that too much of anything is sure to get you in trouble. This view does not hold that all the world is a necessary balance of each component, just that too much law or chaos are dangerous. This is the essence of the axiom, "everything in moderation."

Ethical Neutrality as Opportunistic

Another common interpretation of ethical neutrality is the attitude that characters support laws that serve their personal goals, whether they are good or evil, and work around laws that don't bring profit. These people treat the value of order as being relative to their moral compass. A villain of this type might try to use local zoning laws from preventing a competitor from opening a business in the area; when that fails, she burns down the competitor's warehouse.

When reviewing peoples' views of neutrality on a moral dimension (good and evil), we find even more variations.

Moral Neutrality as Nonjudgmental

According to the AD&D® rules, moral neutrality is a position in which a person refrains from making moral judgments. This imbues a character with the moral faculties of an animal, where actions are driven by instinct. In the case of a morally neutral character, the person may be driven by any number of things, but you can rest assured that good and evil do not enter into the equation.

This kind of attitude manifests itself in a number of ways, all of which create wonderful villains. The first example is the sociopath, a person literally incapable of distinguishing good and evil, but who lives by observing and imitating people around him. The sociopath may even learn to imitate moral behavior, but when other motivations grow strong, everything changes. Sociopaths make good murderers, traitors, thieves, and con artists.

The amoralist is a morally neutral villain who can distinguish between right and wrong, but either *chooses* not to or believes himself above such mundane worries. He sees such moral questions as a shackle for small minds. Amoralists make good murderers. Leopold and Loeb, the Ivy League graduates who murdered a friend simply to have the experience, could be considered amoralists.

The relativist is a morally neutral villain who is so obsessed with open-mindedness and a desire to be nonjudgmental that he becomes morally lazy. The relativist believes that right and wrong are just a matter of point of view, and that if everyone would "walk a mile in the other guy's shoes," there would no longer be *any* conflicts. The relativist never sees himself on any side, but their attitude serves to advance the cause of evil because of their unwillingness to identify and accept its existence. A pacifist who refuses to fight against an invading evil army might be such a relativist.

Moral Neutrality as Selfishness

Morally neutral characters are often seen as people who only act out of self-interest. Whether they act within the law or in spite of

the law is determined by their ethical alignment. This "neutral selfish" character taken to an extreme would be the sort of libertine who would say, "Do what you want as long as it doesn't interfere with me." The neutral selfish always acts in his best interest, regardless of moral implications. Most good characters would view this sort of neutrality as a dangerous form of evil. Neutral selfish villains make good thieves, traitors, corrupt merchants, bards, and small-time crooks.

Villains from Other Alignments

In the following section, we will describe the most likely manner in which a villain could arise from each alignment. The list is not comprehensive. Its purpose is to demonstrate how villains may be hiding in places you might not expect.

Remember that what a villain believes to be his alignment may be at odds with what you, as the DM, know to be the truth. A self-righteous fighter could make offerings at the lawful good temple, then massacre a pack of innocent creatures he believes offended him. He might slowly become an evil person and still believe in his own piety.

Lawful Good

The villainous traits to which the lawful good are most susceptible are intolerance and pride. It is quite possible for a lawful good adherent of a particular religion to quite righteously dedicate himself to the destruction of all that is not good and lawful. Any lawful good king who has started a crusade could be a villain to anyone on the wrong end of his sword. A lawful good villain might also persecute chaotic good characters if he is inflexible in his definition of order. Pride becomes a fault of the lawful good when he arrogantly supposes he knows what is best for others, and subsequently coerces obedience.

Neutral Good

This alignment is the least likely to breed villains. The neutral good tends to be a "good Samaritan." He works within the system to do the "right thing," but at times he does the right thing regardless of what is allowed by the system. A villain is likely to arise out of this alignment only if directly wronged.

Chaotic Good

These characters can be at risk in believing that their ends justify their means. Freedom fighters or terrorists might be chaotic good villains by becoming terrorists. A vigilante could be viewed as a chaotic good villain.

Lawful Neutral

Order supersedes questions of morality for the lawful neutral character. An inquisitor determined to ferret out traitors at any cost, and a soldier who never questions orders, are examples. Lawyers and judges who value law above justice are also potential villains of this alignment.

True Neutral

These characters make terrific potential villains. They believe in maintaining a balance of all things and refuse to make moral judgments. They can often be found switching sides a conflict. If they are working for the benefit of one side and find that it is winning, they may act as traitors to assist the weaker opponent. Their tendency to support the underdog, regardless of issues of right or wrong, make these characters potentially contemptible to characters of good or evil alignments.

Our earlier example of an arms dealer selling weapons to both sides armies in a protracted conflict would serve as a true neutral villain.

Chaotic Neutral

Placing their own needs above those of society, and being indifferent to moral issues, the chaotic neutral is the perfect sociopath. The con-man is a relatively benign chaotic neutral villain, while the independent professional assassin is a more deadly version.

Lawful Evil

Lawful evil characters use the rules to serve their own interests. Lawful evil villains make terrific bureaucrats. They can run villainous organizations or appear within legitimate institutions. Tyrant kings, evil generals, and mob bosses all work well as lawful evil villains.

Neutral Evil

The perfect opportunists, neutral evil villains do anything to satisfy their personal ambitions and appetites. They are potentially the most dangerous villains because their only law is their will. They play by the rules when it serves their personal interests, and work around the rules when they feel it necessary.

Chaotic Evil

Respecting only power, chaotic evil villains cannot be bothered with rules of law. One example of this villain would be bloodthirsty buccaneers who band together out of a need to defeat a common enemy, and who can remain organized only by a brutal, overbearing force.

A Villain for Every Alignment

Good	The Intolerant Paladin (I'm O.K., you're not so hot.)	The Good Samaritan	The Freedom Fighter (The ends justify the means.)
Neutral	The Lawyer (Don't talk to me about right and wrong, talk to me about what's legal.)	The Traitor (No country should gain too much of an upper hand, not even my own.)	The Con–Man (Laws are for people who need them.)
Evil	The Mob Boss (We're going to play by the rules—my rules.)	The Opportunistic Merchant (I'll work with the system when it serves me; when it doesn't, I'll work around it.)	The Pirate (That which does not kill me makes me stronger.)

This chapter describes some techniques for incorporating a villain into your game. These ideas can be used to introduce new villains, or breathe new life into existing villains.

Milking Your Encounters

> Everywhere we looked, the villagers had been turned to stone. I looked at Muriel and asked, "Didn't you seal the entrance to that basilisk cave?"
>
> "I thought you did," she said.
>
> "Oh, well, guess there's no one to complain about it."

The most benign encounter with your villain can become a Pandora's box of problems for your adventurers.

Every encounter can have ramifications felt far beyond its conclusion. The key to fully exploiting your villains is to learn how to "milk" your encounters. Think of each encounter as a stone thrown in a pond; the ripples will be felt by the PCs again and again. Assume the adventurers kill a marauding bear in a random encounter. Think of ways in which this event might lead to others. The bear could have been the companion of a vengeful ranger. The bear may have been the pet of a local ruler. Perhaps the bear kept mountain wolves from the valley near a local village. Any of these are possible and have long term effects.

When you expand your encounters, you create a feeling of continuity in your game, and a general sense of interconnectivity. Using this approach with your villains makes them even more dangerous. If your party eliminates a villain's guards, isn't he likely to increase his security? If he suspects local villagers, he might exact retribution, killing innocents until the "criminals" step forward. Perhaps he hires

some dangerous mercenaries or summons a beast from the outer planes to replace his fallen men. How might the families of the guards react to the murder of their kindred?

Hero-Created Villains

One exciting way to incorporate a new villain into your campaign is to allow your player characters to create the villain. This approach was used memorably in the creation of Superman's arch enemy, Lex Luthor.

Lex Luthor and Superman began their relationship as friends. They met as teenagers when Luthor disposed of some kryptonite weakening Superboy. In gratitude, Superboy built Luthor a laboratory, and Luthor, in turn, committed himself to discovering a cure for kryptonite poisoning. One day, Luthor created a chemical explosion which caused a fire in his laboratory. Superboy, not realizing that his friend was completely in control of the fire, believed Luthor in danger. He blew out the fire with a puff of super-breath. The fumes permanently stripped away Luthor's hair and drove him insane. He became twisted and vengeful, plaguing Superman and the free world.

This dramatic method can be used to tremendous effect in your campaign. The strategy is to introduce a character whose villainy develops as a direct result of the player characters' actions. This strategy instills the villain with an emotional investment in the defeat of the characters.

More Villain than Victim

In Mary Shelly's *Frankenstein*, the monster is more a victim than a villain. While the villain of your campaign may not appear to be a villain prior to his victimization at the hands of the PCs, his reaction must be completely dispro-

portionate to the "crime" against him. You do not want a situation where someone is justifiably angry at the PCs and takes appropriate steps to rectify the situation. In this case, the PCs have only made an enemy, not a villain.

There are three ways in which PCs can create a villain.

1. Wronging the Villain Unwittingly

This is a case where the PCs have wronged the villain without conscious decision.

> We had just ridden out of town when we heard hooves thundering behind us. We wheeled around to see a strange man charging toward us on a donkey.
> "Fiends! Fiends!" he shouted. "You fiends! When you left town one of your horses kicked a stone which broke my window! My wife went to the window to see what happened, and while she wasn't looking my little daughter wandered out of the house and fell in a well! She likes it so much in there she refuses to come out! Argh! I will stalk the forests and hills until I have wreaked my revenge."

This is the weakest method because it minimizes the player's involvement and feeling of responsibility for the villain's creation. The players are more likely to be annoyed and feel tricked by the DM than filled with guilt.

2. Poor Decisions, Unanticipated Consequences

In this case, the player characters make a conscious decision which unintentionally results in the villain's victimization. The example of Lex Luthor's relationship with Superman falls into this category.

> Lord Malor looked up at us from the tattered form of his wife. Our cleric, Adros, continued to hopelessly try to mend the wounds we had inflicted on her.
> We had responded to the lord's urgent plea for help, but did not know the reason for the call. When we approached his manor, a hulking wolflike creature had darted behind the house. We assumed we had been called to rid the manor of a werewolf and gave chase. After killing the beast, we announced ourselves to our host. We quickly learned that we had killed the man's wife, and that he had called on us to enjoin our cleric to cure her lycanthropy.
> As Adros continued to murmur his pious prayers, Malor's face became mottled. He stood stiffly, his hands shaking, and turned away from us.

This method is more effective than the first. While the incident was an accident, it occurred as a direct result of a questionable decision made by the heroes. This is especially potent if the heroes feel they not only made a mistake, but used poor judgment. If they can be tempted into doing something they consider to be wrong, the existence of the villain becomes a reminder of their crime.

3. Intentionally Wronging the Villain

This approach is potentially the most powerful. In this method, the players make a decision which they understand will have a negative impact on the villain. This is best set up as a choice between the lesser of two evils, in which the player characters are not happy about their decision but consider it the best option.

We had to shout above the torrent of the flames. The forest was ablaze. I wiped the soot and sweat from my forehead and shouted hoarsely at the druid: "Look, Darian, it's our only hope to stop the fire before it reaches the village. We have to create a fire wall by burning the sacred grove."

"No!" he bellowed. "You must be mad. You lied to me. You said you would help protect the forest, not destroy it!"

"If we don't burn this grove, the whole valley will be destroyed."

"You can't! This grove is as old as the gods," he sputtered, looking around wildly. "People come and go. Cities of men rise and fall, but the grove has stood by it all. You can't destroy it."

As if making a decision, Darian looked at me sharply and began to recite an incantation. I nodded to Adros, who brought his cudgel down on the back of the druid's head. I paused a moment before passing the flasks of oil to the rest of the party.

In our example, a raging forest fire threatens a small community. The PCs know that if they set fire to the sacred grove of a druid, it will serve as a firewall and save the town. They decide to burn the sacred grove. The druid might never recover emotionally, and may evolve into a bitter villain who hates humanity.

Using the Techniques

While we have shown a number of ways that PCs may slight a potential villain, we have not approached the villain's creation and growth. You need to first identify the *defining moment*. This is the moment the player characters earn the enmity of the villain. Next, we will describe how to orchestrate the newly created villain's return. This is typically the first time the new villain is revealed. We will also explain how to launch your villain's plot for revenge. Beyond that point, your player-created villain run in the same manner as any recurring villain.

Harvesting the Defining Moment

The player's sense of responsibility for a villain's creation is tied to the degree to which the players feel the villain's misfortune might have been prevented. It is very difficult to set up an encounter in which the players are not coerced into mistreating a potential villain. They most often feel tricked.

When left to their own devices, players provide plenty of opportunity to create villains; you just have to be ready to respond. Random encounters can be a rich mine of would-be villains. Players tend to be less "delicate" in random encounters than in encounters they know are important to the scenario. The key is to make notes of your random encounters after every session, and determine if your players may be creating new enemies. If you have a potential villain, develop the character through the steps of character creation described earlier.

In a planned encounter, never force the players to choose the path resulting in the genesis of the villain. When the adventurers were called to Lord Malor's manor and spotted a lurking werewolf, they might have first stopped at the house to warn their host. He could have explained his dilemma and asked that the PCs help subdue his wife and *then* work to cure her lycanthropy. When the heroes were fighting the forest fire, they might instead have thought of a clever use of magic to eliminate the threat. The party would have made a lasting friend instead of creating a villain.

Be patient. Your players will eventually play into your hands. You don't need to push them.

The Return

Players will generally have no idea they have created a villain. The villain's return is likely to be the adventure in which the players first realize their mistake.

The PC-created villain must be a recurring character to qualify for villain status. The return of the villain can be a distinctly gratifying encounter. As long as the villain has a career in evil, the players will feel responsible for his crimes and usually try to prevent them.

The return of the villain should not occur immediately after the defining moment. It is usually best to let one full adventure pass so the players have put the incident out of their minds. In addition to heightening the dramatic effect, the passage of time can be used to explain the new villain's acquisition of power. Use your own judgment regarding how much time is appropriate before the villain returns.

If you think your villain may make a good recurring villain at a later point, make his first plot something other than revenge against the player characters. By making your new villain responsible for a conspiracy *not* targeted at the player characters, you establish that this character is a villain and not merely an enemy. The return ensures that the character is more villain than victim.

The new villain may begin an open career of depravity, hide at the center of a mysterious weblike plot, or collaborate with an established villain. After his experience with the cleric Adros, Lord Malor would be a natural collaborator with Bakshra, who has committed himself to extinguishing religion. Then again, Malor's career might start on another path.

Adros said, "I heard the strangest rumor in the tavern. Seems some mad lord back in Tilltum has begun to purchase human slaves from the drow of the hills. They say he went mad when his wife died without leaving him an heir, and he plans to 'father' an army."

"I'll say it sounds strange," I concurred. "Well, that's not our worry. Let's get back on the road, or we'll never get to the festival before nightfall."

"I'd forget the festival, if I were you. They say the man is Lord Malor."

Malor has done nothing to hide his ambitions. The players' sense of responsibility for Malor's state brings them back to his domain despite their other plans.

The player characters might have stumbled upon a less obvious problem, and eventually found their enemy at the center of a mystery.

It had been over a year since we passed through the valley. We still spoke of the great fire we barely stopped before it reached the village. We approached the town, which seemed oddly quiet. The hills were vibrant with new growth. It was amazing how quickly the forest grew from the ashes.

The main road was overgrown with grass, and scrub grew where there had once been well-beaten trails. The fields were empty, and the buildings looked as if they had been abandoned.

We dismounted, split up, and moved silently through the town, exploring each building. Everything seemed normal: clothing was hung on pegs, salted meat still hung in the cellars. We couldn't tell how long it had been since the townspeople left, but it could not have been too long or looters would have taken everything.

> Adros shouted pointed to a clearing. Scattered in a field of wild flowers were the moldering remains of the townspeople. Most of the bones had been picked by scavengers.

After pursuing this mystery, the party eventually discovers that the druid, Darian, decided man has upset the balance of nature. He has dedicated his life to wiping out the blight.

The Plot for Revenge

When the new villain's first conspiracy is foiled, the heroes may return to their quests and ambitions. If the villain has survived the first adventure, he may begin laying more villainous plans to destroy the player characters. As we said earlier, the villain must be well established before moving to revenge. However, the plot for revenge can be a fun change of pace from "normal" conspiracies.

In Ian Fleming's *From Russia With Love*, the communists decided to eliminate James Bond and destabilize the British Secret Service in one fiendish plot. Half the fun of a revenge plot targeted at the heroes is determining how the villain will set them up *and* how it satisfies the villain's appetite for vengeance.

The Setup

The method of eliminating the PCs is different for every villain. One villain may simply put a price on the heroes' heads. Another might hire the party (using a false name) to lure them into a trap.

The Execution

Some villains have made a career focusing on methods of revenge. In the *Abominable Dr.*

Phibes, the doctor kills each of the physicians he deemed responsible for the death of his wife in a manner corresponding with the Biblical plagues of Egypt. One man's head was crushed at an extravagant costume party while he was wearing a frog mask. Another died by being eaten by locusts.

While colorful forms of revenge can be entertaining to create, a villain should use methods consistent with his character. While one villain may be satisfied with humiliating the PCs, another may not feel content until the heroes are tortured to death. Imprisonment, banishment, and disfiguration are also possible forms of revenge, as is "framing" the characters for a crime. Entire books have been published that compile ideas for exacting revenge.

Of the villains we know well, we can safely say that Bakshra would probably kill someone outright or send his Bloodhounds to kill him. If he was feeling particularly vindictive, he might have the victim subdued and brought to Dranthen Tower to be released in the hunt he usually reserves for clerics. Lady Silith, the medusa, would obviously *petrify* her enemies. Although we have not fully detailed lord Malor's character, he might find a way to curse the heroes with lycanthropy.

Darian, the bitter druid, could take a different tack entirely.

> I quickly rode back to the valley. Adros and the others had left two weeks before, planning to stop to the druid Darian once and for all. The evil druid had single-handedly spread more death and disease than a plague of rats. I decided to move off the road to avoid attracting unnecessary attention.
> As I passed though the lush undergrowth, I suddenly came upon a stand of sturdy oaks. At the site of the druid's burned sacred grove, a glade now grew,

surrounded by ancient trees that had not existed before the fire swept through.

My horse bucked as several crooked figures shambled toward me. From the shield one dragged, I immediately knew that these charred racks of bone and flesh had once been my friends. It looked as if they had died by fire and been set here in undeath as guardians.

I could not allow them to endure this fate. I untied my horseman's mace and kicked my horse forward.

A Mature Campaign Villain

If the villain has survived the trip from his defining moment through development, his return, and his revenge, you can treat him as you would any recurring campaign villain. Rest assured that your players will always have a special relationship with a villain they themselves unleashed.

Villain as Servant

Budlugg crouched over the small wooden chest and examined it carefully. Once he was convinced it held no traps, he set to work with his thieves' picks. The lock sprang easily, and the wooden lid swung open. To our surprise, a small girl in a turban and robe stepped out of the impossibly small chest.

"Thank you, master," she said, smiling at Budlugg. I kept my sword drawn.

> "Uh, hullo. Um, who are you?" was all our thief could muster.
>
> "I am Asoozel. I am a genie and your servant until I have repaid your kindness!" the girl answered merrily.
>
> "That's really not necessary, Sooz," I started. "If it's all the same to you, we'd just as soon let you go and be off. Thanks though!"
>
> The little girl glared at me in a way that chilled my blood.
>
> "Wait a minute," Budlugg protested, "she's my genie, not yours."
>
> "That's right, Budlugg! You tell him," the little girl urged, stepping to his side.
>
> I had a very bad feeling about this.

A number of situations can place put a villain in the service of the party. An interesting story can develop when a trusted servant proves to be a malign force. The villainous servant can take the form of a treacherous human hireling, or even a monster. The advantage of using monstrous servants is that they have a threatening, natural source of power.

Servant as Traitor

Literature and history are full of servants who betrayed their masters. In a role-playing game, a smattering of spies and traitors infiltrating the player characters' party adds spice to any adventure.

A traitor works best as a minor villain who serves the interests of the main villain (we will discuss player characters as traitors in another section). A minor traitor can take many forms, from a henchman of the noble, to the noble himself. If you are going to use this strategy, be certain you know the traitor's specific objectives, and how the traitor communicates with his true masters (if necessary). Keep in mind that you have to allow for the possibility that the PCs will discover the traitor; crucial plot points should not depend upon spies who may be uncovered before playing the role you have planned.

Servant as Monstrous Entity

A malign monstrous entity can come under the real or imagined control of a party in many ways. A number of magical spells allow player characters to summon unwilling servants from other planes. Traditionally, the spellcaster who summons the creature does so intentionally, knowing the servant may attempt to corrupt its instructions or, if it breaks free, destroy the spellcaster. This creates interesting complications. The potential damage such a servant can render from vaguely defined commands is nearly unlimited. An engaging twist on this approach might be to allow the spellcaster to summon something other than what he expected.

In our example, a small genie in the form of a human child was freed by the player characters. What if this charming little person is a tanar'ri from the Abyss sent to the Prime Material Plane on a mission, or perhaps as a punishment? What if the tanar'ri must accomplish a specific objective, such as tempting a player character to change his alignment to evil? The tanar'ri knows the adventurers will be suspicious of its presence and decides to adopt a friendly, even obsequious manner.

An exciting theme of an adventure can involve the party's slow understanding that they have access to a powerful, but evil, servant. *The Lord of the Rings* developed this theme; Frodo was tempted use the One Ring,

while also struggling to destroy it.

The tanar'ri could promise to serve the spellcaster, but as is the case in any agreement with an evil entity, the tanar'ri always attempts to distort its instructions. As the creature insinuates itself into the good graces of the party (and almost assumes the role of a mascot), the PCs may realize they are in "command" of something malign.

The angry villagers had chased us to the treeline before finally turning back. The whole time we ran, Asoozel giggled merrily, kicking Budlugg, who carried her on his back. As darkness overtook us, we paused to rest.

We sat silently while Budlugg paced. Finally, he broke the silence, "Asoozel, you can't erase peoples' faces."

"But you said she talked too much."

"Yeah, I know what I said, but you can't be doing that! Look, I don't want you to do anything without asking me first!"

The girl's lower lip began to quiver and she sniffed back tears.

"I thought you would be glad," she whimpered.

"I'm sorry, 'Sooz. I know you meant well, it's just that…"

Budlugg crouched in front of her and wiped away her tears. I couldn't take it any more.

"Look," I shouted. "I'm not buying this weepy little girl act. You've been doing these things deliberately, and who knows what else you've done that we don't know about. Get out of here!"

Asoozel hugged Budlugg in fright, then looked at me over his shoulder. Her eyes glowed bright red, and a reptilian tongue darted from between rows of razor sharp teeth. She made a gesture in the air and

---

spoke softly in a way that sounded as if she were speaking directly into my ear: "You wouldn't want me to go anywhere, now, would you? You know I only want what's best for everyone, don't you?"

I felt light-headed for a moment, then realized she was right.

The servant might grow in power each time it is commanded and the party overlooks the negative consequences. Eventually, the PCs find themselves wrestling to dispel their servant, who now refuses to leave and may be strong enough to dominate the player characters themselves. A villainous servant traveling with the party can turn a minor initial encounter into an ongoing series of challenges.

Party as Servant

The paladin knelt before the abbot in penitence.

"So, Conner, you would make your own law? You have the arrogance to believe that you know what is best, and what is not? This is the third time you have chosen the path of chaos above the path of law. You have not learned that even when it is most difficult, it is most important to abide by my teaching."

"Only name the task, good abbot, and I will do my penance," Conner whispered.

"You'll have your penance, my willful one. I compel you to travel to the halls of Fzoul Chembryl, black priest of Bane. There, you are to submit yourself to his service. You will perform three tasks for the dark priest. If you perform any evil act in the execution of these tasks, you will lose your paladinhood. We will see if your talents for twisting the word of law serve you there."

A fun and refreshing change of pace can be found in an adventure based upon a party bonded to serve a villain. As penance for the crime of murdering his family while suffering from madness, the oracle of Delphi sent Heracles to her cousin, King Eurystheus of Mycenae. Heracles was required to perform whatever tasks the king demanded. These nearly impossible tasks are immortalized as the "twelve labors of Heracles."

Any number of plot devices can place the party in the service of a villain. The players may be hired as unwitting dupes, pressed into service, or magically bound.

Party as Hirelings

It is not necessary for a party to realize that they are in a villain's service at the outset of an adventure. In fact, it can be fun to watch the slow dawning of recognition as the group realizes its boss is not a very nice person. If the group was coerced into service, the players will have a different attitude when the adventure starts. Whatever the circumstances, a few rules of thumb should be followed when subjecting PCs to this particular torture:

1. Never Force Evil Actions

Even though the party may be in the service of a villain, it is not necessary to make them direct participants in acts of villainy. A villain may hire the party to retrieve an artifact from an abandoned mine. How they accomplish this is left to the group.

2. Give Reasons for Service

If running away is an option, the heroes may not stay around long enough to enjoy the adventure. They may simply rebel, resist, or give up. Having the villain release a hostage or lift a curse when the party completes the task provides a good incentive. The risk of a *geas* spell is that players don't always feel responsible for acts their characters commit under magical compulsion. The advantage of a *geas* spell is that the players know that if they fulfill the letter of the agreement, they are freed from the spell's power.

The Party Bound

An interesting variation on this theme is to have the party bound to execute orders which they must reinterpret to avoid doing evil. Whether by a *geas* spell or simply their binding word, a group of lawful adventurers can be sent on a series of missions where they must execute an evil being's instructions to the letter, but not necessarily the spirit, of the agreement. This can be a fun strategy when the party has been captured by a villain or purchased as slaves. A group enslaved to an evil priest might be given a chance to earn their freedom through "special" service.

When binding the party to a villain, a few additional considerations should be taken into account:

1. Build in Loopholes

When sending a crew into binding agreements with a villain, be sure to include loopholes in their orders. It is no fun for a group to be ordered to kill a bunch of innocents for the benefit of the villain.

You should also be flexible. Like any good puzzle, your players are likely to come up with a solution that you never anticipated. Try not to make a solution too obvious; the players will feel more clever if they had to work to find an answer. The following are

some examples of binding agreements with gaping loopholes.

> Dear Bondsmen,
> As you know, I am campaigning for a position as high consul of the Senate. The upstart do-gooder Thaddeus is threatening the certainty of my victory. Do whatever is necessary to eliminate his threat to my victory.

The party may now work to discredit their master by publicly exposing his villainy. Thaddeus presents no threat to his victory; in fact, there is no danger of him being victorious at all.

> Dear Slaves,
> Bring me the head of my enemy, the duke of Sylvandale, before the moon is new.

The group has promised to bring their master the head of the duke, but they have not promised to leave the rest of him behind. The PCs may now run to the duke and convince him to muster an army to march upon the fortress of their master.

> Darling Thralls,
> The abbot of the lawful good monastery of Lakemont is causing trouble for me. Eliminate the abbot of Lakemont.

The group might go to the seat of the lawful good church and attempt to have the abbot elevated to the position of bishop, and given more men and resources. Having done so, the characters will have effectively eliminated the abbot's position.

2. Include Security of Release

The PCs must believe that the villain will honor an agreement, even if twisted in execution. Consequently, this only works with a magical bond or a villain with an established history of lawfulness. You can even introduce an evil entity, like a dark god, that magically binds the party for the benefit of the villain. The binding entity might be satisfied, even amused, with the PCs' fulfillment of the contract, and release them though the villain is unhappy with the outcome.

Twisting Instructions

Without a precedent being set for twisting contracts, the players might not think to twist the meaning of their instructions. A friendly NPC can gently nudge the PCs toward this approach. The villain himself may have established a propensity for taking liberties with the intent of contracts.

Allying with the Villain

> I remember that dog. Our healer found it wounded on a path in the forest. He nursed it back to health, and it followed him everywhere. The thing was a telepath. The healer was a pacifist who would not harm a creature, even in self-defense, using only an enchanted whip that stunned attackers. What he didn't realize was that, as they traveled, the dog would double back and feed on the stunned creatures the healer left in his wake.
>
> The dog had a great scheme. Few people would raise arms against a healer, so the dog's safety was secure as long as they traveled together. Where else could the dog find an endless supply of food?

Trouble finally started when one of our party fell in battle. The dog was left behind with the wounded woman as a guard. No one knew the dog loved human flesh more than any other meal.

We returned to find that our friend was dead. The dog made up a story of attacking monsters, but we realized it was behind the ghastly crime. We prepared to destroy the dog when it made a desperate appeal to the healer.

"I could not help myself," it lied. "Please understand, I am a beast. I was overwhelmed by instinct. I have tried so long to control myself. I need your help. I need your help if I am ever to gain mastery over my instincts."

The healer bought the dog's story and stepped forward to its defense. We agreed not to kill the dog, but demanded that it leave the party. The healer nobly declared that if the dog had to leave, he would also. We bid the two farewell. Last I saw him, the unwitting healer was still traveling with that murderous beast, leaving a trail of bloodshed.

Another interesting situation arises when a party of adventurers must ally with their enemy. This alliance generally takes one of two forms, both of which can provide an exciting basis for an adventure. The first approach is one in which a party has made an alliance without knowing they are dealing with a villain. In the second approach, the players must ally with a known villain and enemy of the party.

A Nice Guy at the Time

It is challenging for a party to slowly discover that an ally is actually a menacing villain. In our example, a healer allied with a bestial opportunist. The dog's intelligence allowed it to prey upon the healer's sympathy and divide the party. The group was assured that it had been traveling with a monstrous villain, but the healer may never learn.

The villain can occasionally consider the heroes as his allies, directing his depravity toward enemies of the PCs. This kind of relationship is usually revealed through a conflict of interest between the villain and the party. Our example of the dog fits this description. The dog was smart enough to hide its feeding practices from the party that provided it with security and free meals. It was only when the dog's hunger overwhelmed its better judgment that its opportunism revealed villainy (though it still came out of the situation well).

The PCs have special problems if their affiliation with the villain is widely known. They can have as much work cut out for them stopping the villain as clearing their own names.

After several years of adventuring, we decided to devote ourselves to the good church Gonroll. We formed the Knights of Gonroll, and our standard emblazoned with the just hammer of Gonroll, struck fear in the hearts of evil.

Pengo was a fearless fighter we took with us after his town was destroyed by raiding goblins. He was valiant, helping us drive the goblins from the territory. He returned with us to the king's court, where we were recognized for our valor. At that point, he took leave of us and declared that he would return home to rebuild his town.

A year later, we rode to find him. We were planning an attack into Bakshra's territory, and needed all the good fighters we could find. He readily joined us and showed an enthusiasm for the bloodshed

which made our most seasoned men uncomfortable. During the campaign, word reached us about how Pengo had been ruling his village with an iron fist in the name of the Knights of Gonroll. He had killed or enslaved the citizens who refused to convert. No one had said anything to us because they thought he acted with our intentions. When we broached the subject with him, he accused us of heresy and fled the group.

Stories continue to reach us about a band of bloodthirsty knights serving Gonroll. We are never certain of the reception we will receive when we travel, but we must find him. We must stop him.

We Have to Work with *Who*?

More excitement can be generated when you send the player characters into a situation where they are forced to cooperate with a known enemy. As in the case of a rival, the villain may be competing for a common objective.

Sharing a Goal

At times, a villain can share a common goal with the heroes. Trapping the heroes in a tight spot with the villain, where their lives are in danger unless they cooperate to escape, is always a strong common goal.

We were trapped in a box canyon, only to find that Pengo and his men were caught as well. We had advanced miles into Bakshra's territory before being forced down into the ravine. Our old ally had been following the same path to Bakshra's tower and made the same mistake. Bakshra's soldiers began entrenching their position. By nightfall, it would be almost impossible to escape—unless, of course, we worked with Pengo.

Different Objectives Require Cooperation

A common enemy can force adversaries to cooperate. In *Midnight Run*, a bounty hunter and an embezzling accountant were forced to cooperate to avoid the F.B.I. and the Mafia.

"We're here for you, Pengo," I shouted. "We are going to take you back to the church for trial."

"Not likely," he replied. "With Bakshra's men surrounding us, neither of us are going anywhere."

"If we don't cooperate, we'll all die. Give me your solemn vow that you will return to the church with me when we leave."

He sneered. "Let's get out of here first and see who's alive."

Competing for a Goal

While this is the more traditional role of the rival, a villain may act as a rival for one encounter or an entire campaign. A villain may cooperate with a hero even when in competition. Many adventures built around time-dependent races feature a scene where the hero and villain are forced to cooperate.

The staff of Molloth lay in the cavern beyond. Pengo and I were the first ones who had made it this far. I knew that if he gained the staff, his knights would gain ascendancy, and we, the true knights of Gonroll, would be lost. I also knew that if we did not work together, neither of us would escape alive. Pengo had fallen down a small fissure and I had to save him.

"Come on. Climb up, Pengo," I said. "I'll hold the rope steady."

Putting your PCs in a situation where they must cooperate with an adversary, or where they discover that a trusted ally is actually a brutal villain, adds an interesting dynamic to any adventure.

Villain as Tempter

Bakshra looked at me from across the table. Two of his Bloodhounds stood guard at the door.

"I am going to let you go," he began, "but before I do, I want you to consider something. I know you are an intelligent man. You have mastered the arcane art of wizardry. I believe that you are unchallenged. You have no peers. No one else truly understands your passion for learning, and the wonderful products of the disciplined imagination." I felt uncomfortable, but could not help but flush with pride, even when I knew the man who flattered me was a fiend.

He continued: "I would like to extend an offer. I can provide you access to the library of Fallor. You must tell me about the movement of the church's forces. You would not be telling me anything that I could not find out easily elsewhere, but I need someone I can trust."

I barely heard his words. The library of Fallor was rumored to be the single greatest collection of magical research. Fallor had built his archives from the funds of six empires. Although Bakshra was our enemy, I knew that the knowledge in that library would ultimately benefit the church more than anything I might tell Bakshra. Besides, I could always lie.

He removed a ring from his pocket and said, "I would like you to think about it. I want no decision from you tonight, but I would like you to take this ring as a parting gift. I am told it is enchanted. Go now, and if you would like to visit the library, you can use the ring to let me know."

I grabbed the heavy gold ring, and felt foolish for revealing my enthusiasm.

An interesting role for a villain is that of the "tempter." This book begins with the quote, "Virtue untested is innocence." Like Darth Vader, who beckoned Luke Skywalker to the dark side of the Force, your villain can play an interesting role enticing your player characters to commit unwise acts, or acts contrary to their alignment or beliefs.

It is not necessary for your villain to convince a PC to betray his friends. In fact, if the villain can get the PCs to believe that the ends of their actions justify the means, he may eventually get them to completely compromise their convictions.

The Cost of Compromise

Tempting the PCs works best if there is a cost to the PC for such a transgression, and if there is a benefit to the villain. Some villains may want to have the heroes succumb to temptation. This is particularly true for evil creatures from the outer planes.

The RAVENLOFT® campaign has a wonderful device for luring player characters toward evil acts. The Ravenloft Powers check is a roll made by the DM whenever someone performs an overtly evil act. If the check fails, the character gains both supernatural rewards and punishments as the land feeds upon the character's evil.

The cost to a PC for compromising his beliefs is more clear with characters whose class has an alignment restriction. Paladins and rangers risk losing their class abilities if they commit acts against their alignment. Clerics who receive their spells from a deity may also face such consequences.

The cost of compromise does not need to be specific to a character's abilities, nor does the compromise need to be an issue of alignment. In our example, a character rationalized acting as a spy for his enemy. The ultimate cost may be great as he becomes more deeply entwined in his treachery. At first, Bakshra wanted to make it easy for the character to serve him. Once the character leaks information to Bakshra, no matter how benign, he will be snared. The villain will continue to ply him with magical items and research, never giving him real access to the library. This ensures that the PC has incentive to return. If the PC ever withholds information from Bakshra, Bakshra can threaten him with exposure and restart the cycle. This treachery may eventually cost the player character his friends, his country, his freedom, and, ultimately, his life.

Temptation in the Game

Naturally, it is fun for the players to have their heroes face and overcome great temptation. Many films and books include scenes where a

villain offers the hero great power if he joins the villain's side. You may want to create such moments with no real intention of the villain succeeding. Be careful not to make this attempt too transparent, or it loses emotional impact.

The decision to accept a villain's offer may sometimes remove the PC from the game. For instance, if a vampire offered a player character vampiric immortality in exchange for some service, or if the player character in our earlier example decides to serve Bakshra as his mage, you might need to retire the player character and make him an NPC. This can be fun, especially when a player's new character runs up against the NPC in an ensuing conflict.

If the player character succumbs to the villain's temptation and remains in the game, you might be setting up a terrific quest for redemption of the contrite PC. On the other hand, you may be making a nest for a traitor within the party.

Evil within the Party

Things had been going pretty smoothly for us as we worked our way through the dungeon. Too smoothly, really. Our thief, Brent, seemed to be having an easier time spotting the traps that lay in our path. He had been acting a little odd since prying a big gem from a statue in the entrance to the dungeon.

We reached a descending staircase and headed down. Brent waited behind. When the last of us had started down the steps, a roar of flames and flash of light rose from the head of the stairs. A *fireball* billowed toward us as the door slammed shut. The last thing I heard was Brent's laughter.

A traitorous player character is a delightful twist in any adventure. A player character can become a temporary villain in several circumstances. The player character may be possessed through a spell, such as *magic jar*, *domination*, or *geas*. A player character may also fall victim to a shapeshifting monster, like a doppleganger. A PC could also simply choose to betray the rest of the party, either for his own benefit or to gain the favor of a villain.

Under a Spell

Players resent losing control of their characters to magic; fortunately, most magical controls don't last long. *Charms* and *suggestions* can provide short term control or vague guidelines for a victimized PC. A *geas* spell may set an objective, but it is less likely to control a PCs decisions from moment to moment. A *domination* spell can control a PC to the extent that the controlling villain can ascertain a PCs given situation. The *magic jar* is the most fun; with this spell, the villain literally possesses the body of the PC.

It is fairly easy to overcome a player's resentment associated with the control of a *magic jar*. Once a PC is possessed, have a private discussion with the player, and give him the choice of whether he wants to run the character possessed by the villain. This type of opportunity can be fun for a player, particularly if he has always had a hankering to hurl a *fireball* at his friends.

Gone, but Not Forgotten

The approach of infiltrating a party with a doppleganger is more sensitive than introducing magical control. In the case of a *magic jar*, the player can assume that his character will return (unless the party kills the character before freeing him of the spell). A doppleganger probably means that the player character is dead. If the

doppleganger plans to kill the PC before infil-trating the party, you face a few challenges.

You need to carefully execute the infiltration. First, separate the victim from the party. This can be accomplished any number of ways, but is easiest while the party is recuperating and shopping in a city, as opposed to crawling through a dungeon. Once the doppleganger has completed the infiltration, you can extend the same offer to the player that you would in the case of a *magic jar*: Give the player the choice of running the monster. Explain the creature's objective and give a reminder that the doppleganger has limited knowledge about the player character and might make mistakes. If you have developed the character of the doppleganger as a villain, you might let the player look over the monster's character record sheet. You can allow the PC to run the villain until discovered. You might need to intervene to prevent an overzeal-ous PC from wiping out the whole party.

Business as Usual

The key to success is to maintain the illusion of normalcy within the party. The PCs should not be aware of any difference in the possessed character. The most difficult part of the introduc-tion is the actual moment of transition; if you suddenly call a player out of the room, the other players are likely to be suspicious. Cover the transition with misdirection. Making everyone roll dice, then tell several party members that you will require private conferences is usually effective. When you have the phony conferences with the players who have not been taken over, give their characters a meaningless vision or rumor that gets them thinking of something else. You can also pass notes with meaningless rumors. The victim's note tells him that he is possessed and should behave accordingly until you have a moment to talk privately.

Real Traitors

A player character can willfully betray his friends without prompting. This can be extremely destructive to the fun of the game unless carefully handled.

You don't have to punish players for running mercenary-types loyal only to themselves. On the contrary, it can be fun to have a villain tempt, coerce, or bribe a PC into betraying the party, but this approach should be a rare excep-tion. A party overrun with suspicion finds it difficult to agree to *any* decisions. A particu-larly crafty player may be able to betray his party without his friends' knowledge.

The Villain's Survival Instinct

We stood on the bridge that spanned the dark chasm, the six of us at one end, and Miklo waiting at the other. We had finally trapped him. Zed, our wizard, pushed to the front of the line and thrust a wand toward our enemy. The rod glowed for an instant before a jagged bolt of lightning leapt across the chasm.

Grinning, Miklo took the bolt full in the chest but showed no sign of damage. The lightning jarred a fault in the rock wall. A handful of stones showered down on his head. He glanced up as massive sheets of stone broke from the vaulted ceiling. Before we could react, the bridge tore away from its piers and plummeted into the chasm. Miklo slid to his doom as a cloud of dust and rock blinded us. It was over. He was gone.

In most campaigns, the life expectancy of a villain falls into two general categories: minor villains whose destruction is the goal of an individual adventure, and recurring villains

DMs seem determined to protect despite the PCs' best attempts to eliminate. These patterns are boring, and at the very worst your players will be absolutely frustrated with a bad guy who always slips out of their clutches.

The Villain's Defeat

The goal of many quests is the villain's destruction. This is a fun approach for one-shot adventures. It can also be a good strategy when the villain is a monster without a social life in the campaign world. However, a villain can be defeated without destroying him, making for exciting stories. Subduing, imprisoning, banishing, exposing, and converting villains are all ways of eliminating their threat.

Leaving Your Villain an Out

You should allow your villains opportunities for escape that are appropriate to their intelligence, experience, and situation. Even if the adventurers are hired as bounty hunters, you should not preordain the survival of the villain. If the PCs are invading an especially intelligent villain's stronghold, it is unlikely that he would be cornered unless he grossly underestimated the capabilities of the intruders. On the other hand, a villain's overconfidence, inexperience, or lack of preparation can lead to his demise.

You may be inclined to give a recurring villain a bit of help. Fiction is rife with villains and heroes who mysteriously resurface after "death." Arthur Conan Doyle sent Sherlock Holmes and Professor Moriarity plunging

over a cliff together, only to be forced by reader demand to bring Holmes back. Allowing the villain to escape can temper the players' satisfaction with a victory. If the PCs see their adversary fall into an abyss, but never hear the body hit bottom, they may have the satisfaction of temporarily besting their opponent and thwarting his plans, but this satisfaction is tempered with uncertainty and the knowledge that they must remain vigilant.

The DRAGONLANCE® module series included an "obscure death" rule to reuse villains. The approach was to ensure that a body was never found when a recurring villain was defeated. This tactic must be used with care, or the players will feel frustrated that their victory is repeatedly stolen from them.

Letting Your Villains Die

Occasionally, a DM becomes so attached to a villain that he just can't seem to let go. Allowing powerful NPCs to die can rejuvenate a static campaign as different factions vie to fill the "power vacuum." Killing a major character can also restabilize an unbalanced game. The death of a major villain can also dramatically heighten the emotional intensity of an encounter.

1. Revitalize a Too-Familiar World

Killing a major NPC creates tremendous opportunities for a DM. Consider all of the personal and political aftershocks of such an event. How will the people and groups who relied upon the villain continue to meet their needs?

For example, the ruthless warlord of the land next to the player characters' homeland is finally defeated in battle. Will smooth succession result, or will civil war disrupt the empire? What will happen to the morale of the troops? How will the citizens within the empire react?

How long will it take for someone of authority to assume control? Will his armies disband in disarray? How will the heroes who defeated him be perceived in the other country?

2. Restore Game Balance

Removing NPCs can also restore game balance. Imagine a world with a kindly, powerful wizard who always intervenes in difficult situations. This wizard creates an adventure-killing sense of security. The players would feel that the mage would save their characters in times of trouble. In this case, it may be time to kill off the mage. Conversely, if the wizard is a villain of such dramatic proportion that the adventurers stand little chance of stopping him, it may be appropriate to intervene with a timely disappearance or death.

3. Heighten Emotion

Killing major characters can heighten an emotional moment in your game. The longer the NPC has been in the game and the more involved he has been in the campaign, the greater the impact of his death. The circumstances which surround the death of a major villain can also contribute to the emotional intensity of the event. The proximity of the player characters to the villain's death also has a direct bearing on the players' responses.

If the player characters are directly involved in an old enemy's death, the players may have a variety of reactions. They may feel satisfaction at having eliminated the menace. They might also feel regret that they were not able to reform or convert the villain. They might feel an odd sense of loss that this task is now over. At times, they might even miss their old enemy.

If the player characters are not directly

involved, the death could serve as foreshadowing for the appearance of an even more dangerous foe. Imagine that the Batman learned that the Joker had been killed by some greater evil. He might be torn between his impulse to bring the murderer to justice, his satisfaction that the Joker had finally been destroyed, and his fear of a potential enemy who could accomplished the task he could not complete.

What would be the players' reactions when they learn that an old enemy has died courageously in battle? What if they hear he was running away, and died trapped and frightened? What if he had been sentenced to death and executed by the villain's superior? What if the villain was betrayed, or died in his sleep?

As you can see, varying degrees of satisfaction, loss, relief, and pity are evoked depending on the villain and the circumstances of his death. Use these tools to create adventures that your players will retell as stories in the years to come.

The Villain's Achilles' Heel

Many villains and heroes have been undone by a unique weakness or vulnerability. When the hero Achilles was a baby, he was dipped into the river Styx by his mother to make him invulnerable. She was careless in her work, and overlooked the part of his heel by which she held him. Years later, Paris shot an arrow which struck Achilles in the heel, killing him.

It can be helpful to give a particularly powerful villain an unusual vulnerability. The martians in H.G. Wells' *The War of the Worlds* succumbed to germs, and the Wicked Witch of the West was taken out with a bucket of water.

Giving a villain an "Achilles' heel" can leave the DM an "out" if the villain proves too powerful for the wit and abilities of the player characters. It can also be a terrific objective for a quest.

Imagine a villain who has gained insurmountable power. The party quickly learns that they are no match for this opponent. Then they hear a rumor that the source of the villain's power is a summoned beast from the Outer Planes. The beast can only be dispelled with an ancient artifact rumored to lie deep in the ruins of an ancient city. Bingo! Your villain's Achilles' heel becomes an instant series of adventures.

If a villain is aware of his own vulnerability, an interesting adventure can be built around his fear. Imagine a king who has received a prophecy that he will die by the hand of a blind man. He might slay anyone in the kingdom who could fulfill the prophecy. When the PCs arrive to intervene, the party's mage might blind the king with a *light* spell, causing him to stumble off his castle battlements. In essence, he took his own life, and the prophesy was fulfilled in spite of his villainous attempts to cheat fate. Don't use a prophecy to bring the instant downfall of a villain, but allow the villain's awareness of his own vulnerability to serve as a starting point for the adventure.

If you are going to introduce a villain with a vulnerability, don't leave the key to the villain's destruction lying around his lair. No right-minded vampire is going to have a collection of wooden stakes in his tomb, and no medusa will allow a mirror in her cavern. In addition, these types of villains are unlikely to collect scrolls which undo their method of attack. For example, an undead creature that drains levels has no need for a pile of *restoration* scrolls and a medusa will certainly not collect *stone to flesh* scrolls (unless she has a very specific reason, like un-*stoning* umber hulks to eliminate pesky adventurers).

Magic as an Equalizer

> The beast shuffled forward. As it slid over the fallen soldiers, it absorbed them into its mass. Their arms and faces pressed forward from its gelatinous body. A single probing tentacle coiled from its writhing center and reached toward us.
>
> Budlugg and I looked at one another. "This is bad," I said.
>
> "Hang on! Just a second," Budlugg answered as he reached into his pack. He withdrew a battered wand and held it in the direction of the beast. A white beam vaporized the creature. A mass of bones, weapons, and household objects clattered to the ground.

If you do your job creating a villain, events should turn ugly for the player characters. One of the key ideas that we have stressed throughout this book is the importance of a villain being more powerful than the player characters. While we earlier mentioned the idea of an Achilles' heel to help make powerful villains vulnerable, magic is also a terrific equalizer. When using magic for this purpose, use one-shot items like potions or wands with limited charges. This prevents "magical inflation" from unbalancing your campaign.

If you can make magic available to the player characters, you won't have to worry about a villain growing too powerful. This does not mean that you should have your player characters unseating gods, but you will not need to worry about a slightly disproportionate advantage in the villain's favor.

Redeeming Your Villain

> We had cut our way through the undead hordes of Miklo's army for weeks. We spent another three days battling our way past the traps and spectral guardians of his castle. We had not slept, and pressed onward in the face of exhaustion. We knew each day meant another village falling beneath the shadow of Miklo.
>
> At dusk on the third day, we found his chamber. We kicked open the heavy wooden door to his room. Framed in a window far across the vast chamber sat an elderly man cradling a small figure in his arms.
>
> Miklo looked up slowly. Tears marked his weary face. "She is gone," he whispered. "With all of my power, I could do nothing to help my little girl. Please. Can't you help her?" We circled the wizard and prepared to move in on him.
>
> "It's over," he continued. "She must rest. They all must rest." With that, he swept his arm toward the window, and like sheaves of grain the armies of undead collapsed in waves.
>
> It was, indeed, over.

Once in a very great while, a villain reforms. Even Darth Vader redeemed himself before his death by turning on his master.

The redemption of a villain can be an incredibly dramatic experience for your players, particularly if they have a long adversarial relationship with the villain. The villain's change may be a momentary glimpse of virtue or a complete turnaround. Redemption should be motivated by the actions of the players, or by an evil greater than the villain himself.

A bounty hunter who has trapped the adventurers may decide to let them escape

out of respect for their courage. An old enemy may change his ways, possibly joining the side of the heroes when facing a greater evil. In our earlier example, a wizard whose magic released an undead army recognized his evil when his own daughter died.

Conversion Experiences

The key to a villain's redemption is the "conversion experience." This is the moment when the villain recognizes the error of his ways. This can take the form of a grand gesture, in which the villain is destroyed, but he stops the threat which he already created.

> The umber hulks chased us down the tunnel. Pengo leapt forward, knocking me away from the monsters and pulling my sword from my scabbard.
> "Run! Get out of here!" he shouted. The rest of the party stood uncertainly while Budlugg helped me up. The umber hulks lumbered nearer. Pengo turned toward us and swept my sword in a wide arc, clearing the hall.
> "Get out of here," he bellowed. "If you stay, you'll all die. I can hold them off long enough for you to get to the surface."
> Two more monsters rounded the corner. I signaled for the party to retreat.

In this example, the fallen knight makes a heroic gesture toward redemption. By sacrificing himself for the party, the villain gains sympathy in the eyes of the heroes. A conversion experience can also take the form of an actual life-style change. Ebeneezer Scrooge in Charles Dickens' *A Christmas Carol* was a villain whose life changed after he was threatened with a lonely death.

It is difficult to convincingly work a complete turnaround into a villain's life, but a dramatic experience makes the change more believable. Life-threatening experiences or suffering the wages of his crimes might change a villain. If you want to redeem a villain with this method, use a villain who already has a redeeming virtue. The fallen knight Pengo is a candidate because we already know he believes he serves his good church. Perhaps the high priest of his church could show him the errors of his ways.

> Pengo walked out of the high priest's chamber. We were waiting outside, mulling about in the foyer. He had been with the priest for three days and nights. As he neared us, we could see the stain of tears on his coarse face. The high priest emerged from his rooms and placed a withered hand on Pengo's shoulder.
> "Good knights," the old cleric began. "I want you to meet a Knight of Gonroll. He has endured struggles of the heart much greater than any mere battle. He will now be the leader of the order of the Knights of Gonroll, and he will no longer be known as Pengo. That man is gone. I bid you greet your new leader, Penroll, champion of Gonroll."
> We each took inventory of our thoughts and approached to clasp Penroll's hand. I removed the captain's plume from my helmet and handed it to our new friend.

Admittedly, the example presents a situation that might be especially tough for the PCs. You don't always need to subordinate the heroes to the newly redeemed villain, but such events are possible.

It is more likely that a villain will not change regardless of experience. Villains are

more likely to exploit kindness and sneer at redemption. In the play *Tamer of Horses*, we see something rare for literature, but perhaps more realistic. A young hood is given refuge by a teacher and his wife. The teacher attempts to reform the hood, and while the hood makes a good show of having been reformed, he eventually robs all the houses in the neighborhood. This is a false conversion. The false conversion creates interesting possibilities for role-playing.

> My unit had been riding with Penroll for three weeks in Bakshra's land. Sometime during the third week, Budlugg approached me and whispered, "Captain, he did it again."
>
> "Don't call me captain, Budlugg. Penroll leads us now. What are you talking about?"
>
> "Those prisoners, sir. He killed them. When one wouldn't talk, he killed another."
>
> I had been afraid of this.
>
> I spoke to Penroll about Budlugg's accusation. He assured me there was some confusion. I had to give him the benefit of the doubt, but I am uncertain. The party clearly believes he is evil.

The false conversion makes a villain especially insidious. A false conversion works best if the players believe that the potential for a turnaround exists within the villain, or the conversion experience was sufficiently traumatic to initiate the change.

Conversion is also an interesting way to remove a villain from a campaign.

A Guest-Run Villain

Allowing a player to run your villain is different than having a player running a character under a villain's control. In this approach, you invite a guest player to adopt the role of the villain for the length of the session. It is best used at the climax of an adventure, when a party has found the villain and is ready for a showdown.

Give your guest player the background and statistics for the villain, maps of bases, and lists of henchmen or resources. Give the player only the same information normally possessed by the villain. If the villain is not expecting an attack from the player characters, don't let your guest role-player prepare the villain's defense for the attack.

A guest-run villain is best used when the adventurers are heading into close contact with the villain. For example, if a group of adventurers has traveled through an extensive catacomb or fortress for several sessions, and you know that the group is about to stumble upon the villain's lair, you might stop the session before they open the last door. You could begin the next session when you have your guest player available.

The risk of introducing this method too early is that the villainous player is not involved in much of the action. This results in split moderation where you have to run from room to room, asking different groups of players about the actions of their characters. It can also lead to boredom for the villain's player.

When carefully planned, a split session can be entertaining. Provide puzzles to occupy players while you are working with another group. Alternatively, you can use an assistant DM to moderate combat while you deal with other issues.

Raising the Emotional Stakes

Like every conductor of a symphony, director of a movie, or author of a book, a DM's greatest hope is to engage his players' emotions. Whether the mood of your campaign is lighthearted and silly or somber and dark, your players should care about the outcome of their conflict with your villain.

There are a number of ways to engage your players' emotions so they won't want to wait for the next session.

Suffering

> We couldn't believe our eyes. The Lion's Pride Inn was in shambles. Blood streaked the walls and broken pottery littered the floor. Our dear friend Bailey's lifeless body swung from a rope, tied to the cross beam of the dining hall. Upstairs we found the bodies of his wife and children. It took hours before we could make sense of what happened.
>
> Bailey had apparently driven a drunken vagrant from the inn the week before. In the alleyway outside, the man collapsed to the ground in a knot. Bailey approached to help the man to his feet, but was knocked on his back as a slavering beast vaulted toward him from where the man had cowered. It scrambled into the forest, but not before rending Bailey's neck.
>
> His wife had bandaged the wound, and he had rubbed it with wolfsbane. The blood on the walls testified to the futility of his werewolf cure. On the full moon, Bailey slaughtered his family. Regaining his human form in the morning, he was overwhelmed with grief and hung himself.
>
> We heard the vagrant was last seen near Tinnerton.

Players react strongly to a villain responsible for widespread suffering. The more personal the hardship, the more intense the players' reaction. Adventurers frequently shoulder their share of difficulty, so it is more dramatic to direct the suffering at a close friend of the player characters. The old Mafia strategy of punishing a person's family rather than the person himself can be very effective in a role-playing setting. It also helps if the suffering is unjustified.

In our example, a longtime friend of the PCs is stricken by the abominable curse of lycanthropy and slays his own family while transformed. This sort of episode is certain to stir the hearts of your players and send them in pursuit of the villain who caused the suffering.

Players are inured to the typical slings and arrows of the adventuring life. Consequently, if you want the PCs to suffer rather than their friends, you need to do more than deliver heaps of damage. The RAVENLOFT® campaign makes extensive use of curses, which can be excellent paths to laying a difficult but interesting burden on the character. These curses are often targeted at a character's interests. If a bard has a great love of music, he may lose his hearing. A greedy thief may awaken to find that he can only sustain himself by eating gold, and is forced to consume his treasure to survive.

Targeting a player character's health as a means of causing him to suffer has little emotional impact. Players are pretty comfortable with the cycle of having their characters go out to get beaten up, then return home to get healed. Even diseases and "common" curses are taken in stride as long as there is a powerful church nearby where heroes can exchange healing for completion of a quest. The loss of a key ability score or favored spell has a greater effect on a player if the character can never recover the ability or spell. Real loss is much more dramatic than a temporary set-

back. However, a fine line exists between heightening the emotion in an adventure and frustrating the players. Great losses should only be used if the ensuing excitement outweighs a player's initial disappointment.

Surprisingly, many players react strongly to a slight which does not inhibit their playing ability, but effects something less tangible. A villain who cuts a PCs cheek and leaves a scar may incite a greater reaction than a penalty to an ability score. You can also introduce trials of endurance by playing with overlooked rules. What would happen if the group were trapped in a room for two weeks? How long would it take them to run out of food? What if the group was badly beaten and had no magical means of healing? What happens to a party who runs out of water in a desert, or is over-encumbered in a blizzard?

Sacrifice

"We will only defeat it if we know how it thinks," Budlugg insisted.

"I still don't see the point of exposing yourself to the werewolf. What if it kills you?" I asked.

"You will be close enough to drive it off once it bites me. But only after it knows that I'm a lycanthrope will I have a chance of gaining its trust."

"What do we do in the meantime?"

"Lock me up on the full moon," Budlugg answered with a grin.

"This is not worth the risk. We can't bring back Bailey and his family."

"Just be there when I call."

He turned and headed toward the hill.

The single most powerful tool to evoke empathy from your players is sacrifice to a cause. The magnitude of a player character's sacrifice is directly proportional to the character's dedication to defeating the villain. The most severe sacrifices a player character can make are a loss of experience levels or permanent loss of ability scores. Permanent loss of a favorite magical weapon or mount is also a good choice. The key point in designing an effective sacrifice is that the personal cost must outweigh the personal gain. A sacrifice must be voluntary, something you cannot force on the players. You can only create the opportunity.

A character willingly entering a tomb of undead to destroy a powerful lich is taking a personal risk, and if he willingly engages the spectral guardians in combat, he may sacrifice experience levels. On the other hand, if this same adventurer is jumped by a gang of undead who drain his levels in a random encounter, the player will not perceive this as a sacrifice that heightens his commitment to the cause.

A sacrifice by an NPC can also increase the players' commitment to a task. If a friendly elf gives up the opportunity to become the leader of his tribe and chooses to join the PCs on a quest to defeat a villain, the players will feel more dedicated to the cause. If that same elf gives his life so the PCs may continue against their foe, the players will feel a stronger commitment to the goal.

The hardships and necessary sacrifices associated with wilderness travel can also hold emotional impact for your players. Sacrificing a favorite mount to use as food during a hard desert journey is an excellent example.

Danger

> It had been two weeks since the werewolf dragged Budlugg into the forest. We waited for his signal that night, but it never came. We found Budlugg's campsite; only a few traces of blood gave any indication of the struggle. We tried to track the beast, but the hounds refused to follow the trail. We gave up after three nights and returned to wait at the inn for some sign of the creature.
>
> On the fourth night, I stepped outside for some air and walked around the building. As I rounded the corner, I came within two feet of the blood-drenched maw of an enormous wolf. I froze. The beast glared at me and watched. I felt as if it was waiting for me to run, to make any move that would inspire it to tear me to pieces. I began to shake uncontrollably. The creature turned from me in contempt and loped into the shadows. I cannot help wonder if it was my friend Budlugg who had spared me, or a dumb beast sated from a previous kill.

While suffering and sacrifice are good tools to heighten the emotional stakes in an adventure, perceived danger is also a powerful tool. Regardless of whether a risk to a player character is real, a perceived danger is likely to gain their attention.

In addition to exposing the PCs to the multitude of hazards offered by the adventuring life, danger and fear can be evoked by drawing the story away from familiar territory. The least threatening spells can create a feeling of imminent danger; cantrips can cause all of the leaves in a grove to twitch, and an *unseen servant* can create a sense of a mysterious pres-

ence. Illusions, of course, can have tremendous power, and when created by a being who has psionic capabilities or the means to detect the greatest sources of a character's fear, the results can be stirring.

The RAVENLOFT® *Realm of Terror* rules book has many suggestions to heighten fear in an encounter. Many DMs use the classic technique of asking the players to make saving rolls. The DMs pause, root through the rules in concern, roll some dice, and go on without telling the players the purpose of the rolls.

Adventurers deal with danger as a matter of course. It is uncertainty that creates unease.

Warnings and Foreshadowing

> I sat in the tavern and drank for comfort. The rest of the party had gone to bed. A traveler walked in late and ordered a drink from the other end of the bar. For a moment, I swore the bartender looked like my old friend Bailey, the innkeeper of the Lion's Pride Inn. He stood across the bar from the traveler and poured him a drink. The marks of the rope on the innkeeper's neck were as fresh as the day we found him. The ale he poured looked black, spilling on the floor.
>
> I stumbled off my stool. The vision vanished. The traveler eyed me warily, gathered his things, and left the bar without finishing his drink.

The spectral visage of an old friend or relative appears and seems to give a warning. Dogs flee from you in fear. You stumble across three witches in the forest who prophesize that you will be king. An eagle drops a wolf cub from its talons into your hands. All of these are unsettling omens or warnings.

Warnings can be as mundane as rumors of a villain's reputation, or as dramatic as the ghost of your father appearing to finger his murderer. Successful omens must be kept vague so that they do not lock the game into a single outcome. You *can* be specific with a conditional warning, illustrating a doom that awaits *unless* the villain is stopped.

Vague portent might take the form of dogs running from a PC. An old woman may approach and point a finger, accusing the character of defying the grave. The player may get the picture that his character is fated to die. He will know he has beaten his fate when, after driving a stake through a vampire's heart, the neighborhood dogs no longer cringe at his presence.

On the other hand, the group may get a very specific vision of a friend floating dead in a river. A later vision may reveal someone holding the friend underwater. Now the party knows that their friend will be murdered unless they intervene.

A warning does not need to be supernatural. Your villain's reputation (and rumors of his foul deeds) can heighten the adventure's emotional impact. Give some thought to your villain's history. What might people know or think about the villain? Have any of his activities attracted notice? Some of the most common misperceptions contribute to rumors. Most people can recall an elderly neighbor who was believed by the neighborhood children to be a witch. Rumors are notoriously unreliable, and you can have fun planting misleading seeds.

We have used a number of examples throughout this book to illustrate different approaches to creating unforgettable villains. This section presents the example villains used in this book, as well as a few others you may add to your campaign. The compendium includes Darkon, who we met in the section "Recurring Villains." Pengo is introduced in the section "Allying With the Villain." Mervis makes her first appearance, but is an example of a true-neutral villain described in the section "Villains For Every Alignment." Asoozel is a tanar'ri who appears in the section "Villain as Servant." She also provides an example of a villain created from a MONSTROUS COMPENDIUM® entry. Thoto is the bounty hunter used to illustrate "The Rival."

Three villainous organizations are also presented in this section. The Corn Kings provide an example of a villainous network. The Bree is a villainous hierarchy. The Levellers is also a hierarchy, providing an example of how a chaotic good organization becomes a force of evil. Some of the details of both the individuals and the organizations have been left open to allow easy transition into your campaign.

Darkon

Human Male
3rd Level Fighter, 9th Level Thief
Neutral Evil

Strength:	15
Dexterity:	18
Constitution·	8
Intelligence:	5
Wisdom:	17
Charisma:	6
Hit Points:	30
AC:	2

No. of Attacks:	1
THAC0:	16
Damage:	1d8 (w/long sword)
Movement	12

Occupation

Darkon is a former ranger and thief who now serves as the constable and captain of a king's private guard.

Objective

Darkon wants to establish a thieves' guild operating under the protection of his police force. He plans to extort money from local merchants and business people to secure their safety from the thieves (which he controls).

Motive

Darkon is driven by an obsessive need for power. He also has a strong need for autonomy.

Personality

Dominant Trait 1: Sadistic
Dominant Trait 2: Opportunistic
Contradictory Trait: Generous

Darkon seeks any opportunity to increase his personal power or gain advantage over an opponent, using any means to advance his interests. His sadism inspires fear among his subordinates.

Strangely, Darkon is extremely generous, often giving his men the first pick of any loot, and bestowing large gifts to those who serve him or may be of service in the future. Darkon also has the odd habit of making generous gifts of money to his enemies and the families of his victims. He sees wealth as a tool to win men's hearts.

Attitudes and Behaviors

Darkon views people as opportunities or obstacles. His emotional commitment to people only extends to where they might serve his interests. He treats friends and allies with extraordinary generosity. He secured his position at the head of his thieves' guild by only demanding a small stipend from his men. Darkon treats his enemies with a savage cruelty that inspires as much loyalty from his men as his generosity.

Tastes and Preferences

The constable's tastes are refined but not ostentatious. His clothing is always of the highest craftsmanship but not decorative.

Surroundings

Darkon has quarters in the castle with the king.

History

Darkon was raised by his mother, who was a ranger. She spent her life protecting a large stretch of forest near Bunder. Darkon's mother pressured him to pursue a life in the forest. His strange delight in torturing animals was met with increasingly severe punishments, which only seemed to fuel his sadistic nature. He wanted to leave the forest, but his mother was determined that he should learn her craft. After years of resistance, Darkon finally threw himself into the study of wood lore.

Darkon's mother passed away three years later. The young ranger was free from his

mother's watchful eye, and decided to save some money and leave the forest. He applied his mother's teaching to stalk and rob travelers. He enjoyed tracking his prey and ultimately killing them and hanging them upside down like game animals. His abilities bolstered his confidence; each dead body reaffirmed his power.

During his search for money to start his new life, Darkon tracked and cornered a small gang of brigands. He realized that the group would be useful to him alive and gave them the choice to either serve him or die. Two of the thieves lost their lives before the remaining men accepted Darkon as their leader.

After a series of increasingly audacious plans, Darkon's gang eventually became the thieves' guild of Bunder. The guild was eventually driven from the region, and Darkon traveled alone for months before hiring on as a member of the constabulary, which he now leads.

Network

Darkon commands the 20 soldiers of the city's police force. He also commands eight men who serve as the king's personal guard. He has direct access to the king and an increasing number of contacts in the city's underworld.

Appearance

Darkon is large and intimidating, and has coarse manners. His face is ruddy and clean shaven. His red hair is straight and cropped at the shoulder. He smiles only when involved in some bloody act of cruelty. His dark brown eyes are devoid of feeling. He rarely stands straight or still.

Darkon commonly wears forest-green studded leather armor under a tabard embroidered with the royal crest. He wears jack boots, and carries a long sword and hunting knife.

Nonweapon Proficiencies: leatherworking, mountaineering, running, rope use

Darkon spent many summers in his childhood running the forest trails and scaling mountains. Under his mother's tutelage, he gained proficiency with leatherworking and learned to handle rope. With the exception of rope use, these skills have all fallen into disuse, and he makes any proficiency check with a penalty of –1.

Weapon Proficiencies: sling, lasso, short bow, short sword, long sword

Darkon learned the sling and the lasso as a child. His mother taught the basics of swordplay, but he was not adept with blades until he became a robber. Darkon continues to use a lasso; combined with a successful rope use proficiency check, all lasso attacks are made at +2.

Thieving Skills: Pick Pockets: 50%, Open Locks: 67%, Find/Remove Traps: 55%, Move Silently: 60%, Hide in Shadows: 46%, Detect/Hear Noise: 20%, Climb Walls: 65%, Read Languages: 45%, Backstab ×4.

Pengo

Human Male
7th Level Fighter
Lawful Evil

Strength:	15
Dexterity:	14
Constitution:	8
Intelligence:	14
Wisdom:	16

Charisma:	14
Hit Points:	38
AC:	5
No. of Attacks:	3/2
THAC0:	14
Damage:	1d8 (w/bastard sword)
Movement:	12

Occupation

Pengo is a renegade knight and champion of a lawful good church.

Objective

Pengo seeks to convert all intelligent creatures to the faith of the lawful good church, and destroy any who refuse.

Motive

Pengo is driven by a need for order and aggression. He takes any action necessary to eradicate all that is not good and lawful.

Personality

Dominant Trait 1: Intolerant
Dominant Trait 2: Arrogant
Contradictory Trait: Kind

Pengo possesses the worst traits of a crusader. He is completely intolerant of anyone who not good and lawful, and often behaves in a manner befitting an evil chaotic. He is impervious to criticism, and questions the piety of clerics who speak against him.

Pengo is often kind to lawful good people. He has built an orphanage to raise children within the church of Gonroll.

Attitudes and Behaviors

Pengo believes that all races are either on his side or his mortal enemies. He spends much of his time pursuing missionary work. When his efforts do not take root, he exterminates the unconverted.

Pengo is dutifully kind toward those not yet exposed to his truth.

Tastes and Preferences

Pengo takes great pleasure in self-denial. He primarily survives on bread and water. He takes pride in his magnificent and flamboyant plate armor, which he believes exemplifies the glory of his god.

Surroundings

Pengo's base of operations is the small farming town where he grew up and now rules. However, he spends much of his time on pilgrimages, missionary campaigns, and quests.

History

Pengo was raised in a small farming town as an able fighter and competent horseman. He volunteered to assist a band of knights from a lawful good church in an effort to drive raiding goblins from the territory. He was decorated for valor. What he learned of the lawful good religion before his return home satisfied his desperate need for order, which had been aggravated by the loss of his community. He committed himself to rebuilding his town in the image of this lawful good ideal.

Pengo's uncompromising fanaticism and natural aggressiveness turned the town into an oppressive military theocracy. He had no qualms about annihilating neutral and evil

people. He magnanimously condemned the good chaotics to slavery, which he believed would ultimately teach them the value of law and service.

If news of his crimes reaches the lawful good church, he will be brought to trial or excommunicated, in which case it is likely Pengo will no longer recognize the authority of the church.

Network

Pengo recruited a cadre of loyal knights from the surrounding area who assist him in reforming the community. He has acquaintances among the true knights of the lawful good church.

Appearance

Pengo is a tall, thin man with brilliant blue eyes; his expression reflects passion and determination. His blonde hair is cropped short. He carries himself upright with the natural bearing of a military leader.

Pengo wears silver plate mail elaborately decorated with images and symbols of his church. His warhorse's full barding is similarly decorated.

Nonweapon Proficiencies: agriculture, armorer, blind-fighting, animal handling

Pengo became adept at agriculture and animal handling on his family farm. He also learned to construct armor, spending over a year making his own elaborate gear, as well as the barding for his horse. Curiously, all of the children of his town gained a certain proficiency in blind-fighting.

Weapon Proficiencies: bastard sword,

broad sword, horseman's mace, heavy horse lance, mancatcher, composite long bow

Since his boyhood, Pengo played at combat. He could be seen in his family's fields, charging the length of the furrows with a tree-branch lance propped across the neck of a plowhorse. When he became old enough to handle real weapons, he applied himself to a knight's tools of war.

Mervis

Female Human
8th Level Wizard
True Neutral

Strength:	13
Dexterity:	13
Constitution:	16
Intelligence:	17
Wisdom:	14
Charisma:	12

Hit Points:	34
AC:	10
No. of Attacks:	1
THAC0:	18
Damage:	1d4 (w/dagger)
Movement:	12

Occupation

Mervis is a judge and scholar, and is occasionally consulted for diplomatic missions by the king.

Objective

Mervis believes the forces of good have gained disproportionate power and actively works to restore the balance between good

and evil. She believes that by forcibly breeding orcs and humans in the city's jail that she will increase the population of half-orcs. She is convinced that more half-orcs in the community will create a greater tolerance between the bitter enemies of humans and orcs.

Motive

The judge is driven by a strong need for affiliation and understanding. This manifests itself in her desire to be accepted, and accept others regardless of their alignment or agenda.

Personality

Dominant Trait 1: Duplicitous
Dominant Trait 2: Manipulative
Contradictory Trait: Compassionate

Attitudes and Behaviors

Mervis believes in equality. She believes there is room for all creatures and behavior, and that none should gain supremacy to the detriment of others. She tends to side with the underdog in a conflict, regardless of issues of right and wrong, or good and evil. She treats all people courteously.

Tastes and Preferences

Mervis likes to be seen at social affairs. She adopts habits and fashions of other races and cultures to promote her worldly outlook and gain the acceptance of others.

Surroundings

Mervis has a large dwelling filled with bad art and artifacts from various cultures in a fashionable section of town.

History

Raised in the lap of luxury as the only child of an aristocratic couple, Mervis avoided mundane work and buried herself in academic interests. Her extraordinary learning earned her the position as judge; she also had an affinity for magic. She never obsessed over magic, viewing it as an extension of her learning.

Mervis' open-mindedness, combined with her exposure to enemies of the state through the justice system, has led her to betray the king on several occasions. Mervis thinks in terms of the "balance" rather than the individual lives lost through her treachery.

Mervis' father was one of the first to fall to her moral lassitude. He had been a diplomat responsible for extending the influence of the good kingdom. An orc assassin sent from an enemy empire had been caught and brought before Mervis for judgment. She interviewed the prisoner in his cell. During the conversation, she learned that her father was the assassin's target. She came to the conclusion that her kingdom had gained too much power; she figured that an assassin sent hundreds of miles to kill her father indicated an imbalance. She deliberately left open the door's lock to the prisoner's cell. Later that night, her father was found dead.

Network

Mervis is well connected in all levels of society. In addition to having access to the king and his court, Mervis has contacts among her kingdom's enemies and the criminal elements of her city.

Appearance

Mervis has long golden hair which she wears in braids. She is tall and has a pale complexion. Her expression is generally open, interested, and warm. She has an aristocratic bearing and carries herself with confidence. She wears the latest fashions and the odd items she buys in remote lands.

Nonweapon Proficiencies: spellcraft, ancient history, reading/writing, etiquette, modern languages, ancient languages

Most of Mervis' youth was spent in her parents' library. When she was drawn away from her books, it was usually to attend an important social function. Her proficiencies of history and languages, as well as her innate sense of etiquette, aid her in diplomatic work.

Weapon Proficiencies: dagger

Mervis has never had much experience with physical conflicts, and has never actually used the dagger she carries for protection.

Mervis' Spells:
Level 1: *jump, protection from evil, audible glamour, identify, mending, sleep, shocking grasp, detect undead, hypnotism;* Level 2: *summon swarm, improved phantasmal force, protection from cantrips, bind, mirror image, hypnotic pattern, alter self, Leomund's trap;* Level 3: *monster summoning I, blink, flame arrow, hold person, phantom steed, delude, gust of wind, wind wall, clairaudience, item, explosive runes;* Level 4: *solid fog, emotion, stoneskin, massmorph, phantasmal killer, minor globe of invulnerability, remove curse, shadow monsters, wall of ice, shout, Evard's black tentacles.*

Asoozel

Tanar'ri, Lesser—Succubus	
Intelligence:	16
Alignment:	Chaotic evil
AC:	0
Movement:	12, Fl 18 (C)
Hit Dice:	6
Hit Points:	30
THAC0:	15
No. of Attacks:	2
Damage:	1-3/1-3 (fists)
Special Attacks:	Energy drain
Special Defenses:	+2 or better weapons to hit, immune to fire, never surprised
Magic Resistance:	30%
Size:	S (4'4")
Morale:	14

Occupation

Asoozel is a succubus, a lesser tanar'ri who fills the pits of the Abyss with mortals she has destroyed;

Objective

Unlike her sisters, Asoozel does not undo moral men by tempting them with her beauty and draining their energy in passionate embraces. She is committed to luring good and neutral mortals to the side of evil before destroying them.

Motive

Asoozel is motivated by a need for power over the will of mortals, and her innate aggressive desires to destroy good through temptation.

Personality

Dominant Trait 1: Manipulative
Dominant Trait 2: Patient
Contradictory Trait: Mischievous

Asoozel manipulates men, seducing them to rebellion against law and goodness. She has an impish and dark sense of humor, and loves to toy with her victims.

Attitudes and Behaviors

Asoozel believes all mortals are potential fodder for the tanar'ri in their Blood War against the baatezu of the lower planes. She enjoys victimizing humans, finding other races lacking in passion. She treats each of her victims as a close friend and ally. She plays on the character weaknesses of each victim, gaining their devotion and luring them to evil and chaos. She kills her victims by draining their energy.

Tastes and Preferences

As a creature of the lower planes, Asoozel loves her work above all else. She has little interest in material goods, food, or creature comforts except to the extent which they help unhinge her prey.

Surroundings

Asoozel prefers to assume the guise of a genie. She often follows a group of travelers before allowing them to find her old oil lamp. She generally prefers to work in cities for the wide variety of potential victims, but occasionally haunts the retreats and monasteries of devout clerics, who always offer greater challenge.

History

Asoozel is young by tanar'ri standards. From her earliest centuries, she took an interest in forms of seduction beyond the physical. She uses *ESP* to gauge her victim's weaknesses. Asoozel takes great pride in her ability to tempt mortals. In fact, she only uses her spell-like power of *suggestion* or her ability to *charm* people if her plot is jeopardized. She does not refrain from using these abilities on the friends or acquaintances of her targeted victim if it will help push him closer to evil.

When she appears as a young genie to her victim, Asoozel begins by serving her "new master" faithfully, twisting her instructions as the victim grows more comfortable with her presence. She focuses her energy on manipulating her victim's circumstances, making small moral compromises increasingly attractive until the victim realizes that he has committed a murder or some other heinous act. If her victim somehow detects her true alignment, she explains it as part of a curse that is dispelled when she completes her service to her master.

Asoozel enjoys strife and discord in any group with which she travels. She will not start or perpetuate such problems in an obvious manner. She feeds the fires of unrest by reinforcing peoples' discontent beneath a guise of helpfulness.

Asoozel recently (300 years ago) challenged a glabrezu to a contest to determine who had greater mastery over the wills of mortals. The true tanar'ri agreed to the tournament, whose winner will be decided by a nahfeshnee on a throne of flame in the Mountain of Woe. Abrizna, the glabrezu, is in danger of losing the contest, which ends in six months. He may begin to interfere directly with Asoozel's adventures.

Network

Asoozel has gained some notoriety in the Abyss over the last 300 years, but has spent most of her time in the Prime Material Plane. Her only contact with her kind was a balor she once *gated* when she was in danger of destruction. She has also had a few unpleasant encounters with Abrizna.

Appearance

Asoozel is short and prefers to take the form of an 11-year-old human girl. She often appears with a purple turban, beautifully embroidered silk shirt, and billowing pantaloons. Her face is bright and cheerful, and she has large brown eyes.

Special Abilities

Asoozel's statistics are drawn directly from the entry for succubus in the MONSTROUS COMPENDIUM® *Outer Planes Appendix*. She differs from the standard succubus only in her somewhat diminutive size.

Asoozel has the following spell-like powers: *darkness 15' radius, infravision, teleport without error, telepathy.*

Asoozel can use the following powers once per round, one at a time, at will: become *ethereal* (as if using *oil of etherealness*), *charm person, clairaudience, ESP, plane shift, shape change, suggestion*. She may also attempt to *gate* a single balor once per day with a 40% chance of success.

Thoto

Male Half-Elf
6th Level Fighter/6th Level Thief
Neutral Evil

Strength:	16
Dexterity:	17
Constitution:	15
Intelligence:	14
Wisdom:	16
Charisma:	7
Hit Points:	35
AC:	5
No. of Attacks:	1
THAC0:	15
Damage:	1d6 (w/short bow)
Movement:	12

Occupation

Thoto is a bounty hunter and mercenary.

Objective

Thoto does not have a general plan, plot, or conspiracy. He seeks out opportunities to test his mastery of his craft.

Motive

Thoto is driven by an insatiable need for achievement and desire for autonomy. He constantly tests his abilities by pitting himself against dangerous competitors.

Personality

Dominant Trait 1: Competitive
Dominant Trait 2: Arrogant
Contradictory Trait: Superstitious

Thoto is excessively competitive. He considers every job a test of his worth and resorts to any low trick to complete his assignment. His self-confidence manifests as arrogant contempt for competitors or prey he finds unwor-

thy of his effort.

Thoto is extraordinarily superstitious. His life is governed by a hundred odd rules and rituals of his own invention; he has set prisoners free because of his fear of bad luck.

Attitudes and Behaviors

Thoto has no sense of compassion, viewing others as yardsticks to measure his ability. He knows no loyalty beyond the contracts he makes with employers. He has alternately hired himself to two divided parties in a dispute, until one finally gained the foresight to preclude such an agreement in his contract.

Tastes and Preferences

Thoto's tastes and preferences are ordinary, with a number of odd exceptions driven by his superstitions. For example, he always keeps a lock of hair from each of his victims threaded into a belt. He prefers burnt bread, and believes it is good luck to eat some before a hunt.

Surroundings

Thoto avoids the company of others and prefers the trails of the wilderness to streets of a city. However, he rarely passes up the opportunity to appear at large competitions of archery or swordsmanship.

Thoto has a "permanently" rented room in a small country inn which serves as his address.

History

Thoto was orphaned at the age of nine and not adopted because of his mixed blood. He was raised as a squire to a band of mercenaries held together by the forceful leadership of Tung, the strongest member. Thoto thrived in this environment and quickly earned his place among the savage fighters. Tung taught Thoto that loyalty should only extend as far as a patron's purse strings, and that small mistakes can mean death.

When work was scarce, the band ambushed travelers, which developed Thoto's skills as a thief and fighter. Thoto worked his way to second-in-command by defeating each member of the band in combat. Thoto also proved that he had exceeded even his master in cool self-interest by accepting his first commission as a bounty hunter: he betrayed the band to a local ruler.

Thoto built his reputation by accepting contracts of increasing difficulty. He found capturing fugitives alive more challenging than killing them, and inadvertently developed a false reputation for "kindness." In truth, Thoto kills without a second thought. He simply finds the challenge of subduing prey more exciting.

Thoto generally commands a high price for his services, though he accepts interesting work for a nominal amount. He deals fairly with his patrons, but has no qualms about killing a cheat or hiring himself to a former patron's enemy.

Network

Thoto is well-connected with the law-enforcement organizations of various governments who hire bounty hunters. He also knows a fair number of wealthy individuals who have required his services. Additionally, Thoto has a large number of enemies that consists of the countless individuals he has captured for his clients.

Appearance

Thoto has a long scar running down his face from his forehead, across his nose, and down to his chin. His back is marred by lashmarks from

his youth with the band of mercenaries. His hair has receded, leaving a dramatic widow's peak. His face is generally cold and expressionless.

Thoto carries himself with the balance and self-awareness of a cat. He dresses inconspicuously while on a mission. He prefers loose fitting clothes that allow him to hide small tools and weapons. In combat, he wears hide armor and carries a body shield.

Nonweapon Proficiencies: set snares, disguise, bowyer/fletcher, tracking, cooking

All of Thoto's skills serve to make him more independent. He uses his talents for tracking and setting snares to catch both his dinner and fugitives.

Weapon Proficiencies: short bow, short sword, net, bastard sword, quarterstaff, throwing axe

Thoto prefers his short sword and net in close quarters, but he is equally skilled with bow, bastard sword, or quarterstaff. He strikes with the flat side of his bladed weapons to subdue his quarry.

Thieving Skills: Pick Pockets: 70%, Open Locks: 57%, Find/Remove Traps: 45%, Move Silently: 52%, Hide in Shadows: 47%, Detect/Hear Noise: 20%, Climb Walls: 92%, Read Languages: 30%, Backstab ×3.

The Corn Kings

Cult network.

What Do They Deliver?

The Corn Kings are a group of villainous plantation owners who worship a dark god of the harvest. The Corn Kings control most of the arable land in the kingdom. They provide inexpensive grain and corn to merchants and freemen. Their fields are tilled by undead and somnambulate humans. The cult provides a path to wealth and power to the plantation owners, and a quasi-religious way of life for the peasants in their region.

How Do They Acquire Resources?

The Corn Kings obtain their land and labor by coercing the peasant population to give their property to the cult. Resistant landholders are found working in the Corn King fields as zombies. This practice has been so effective that the cult has more land than it requires.

How Are They Organized?

The Corn Kings consist of a dozen prominent land owners. They have no formal hierarchy, but meet to fix prices and plan levels of production. When economic conflicts of interest threaten to divide them, their shared religious values keep them together.

Do They Have an Advantage?

For generations, the families of the Corn Kings have studied wizardly and clerical arts. They use these abilities to coerce small peasant families and landowners to sell their property. The cult employs its dark magic to control the minds of the peasants to build a cheap labor force. Rebellion is quickly quelled, and troublemakers turn up working the fields as undead. This undead labor force works day and night, resulting in lower costs and higher crop yields. No small farmer can compete with the prices of the cult-grown grain.

The Corn Kings evaluate everything in

terms of long-reaching consequences; they can take months or years to make decisions. They have never faced a strong or well-organized resistance, a definite weakness in a confrontation with a new adversary.

How Do They Plan for the Future?

The Corn Kings work together to control the supply and price of their products. They have been very successful in ensuring the prosperity and longevity of their organization. They have recently hired their slaves to other merchants and tradesmen. This program has been met with a variety of reactions ranging from interest to disgust.

How Do They Establish Conformity?

In the rural hills of the kingdom, the cult of the dark harvest god has existed in one form or another for thousands of years. The peasants fear but voluntarily perpetuate the arcane rituals and customs of the Corn Kings.

Seasonal celebrations and sacrifices, as well as regularly observed customs and rituals, contribute to the organization's maintenance. Every family raises their second child to serve in the fields of the plantation masters. The senior members of the cult are revered as shamen, but have no specific authority or rule except to preside over the ritual sacrifices which ensure a good harvest.

How Do They Satisfy Their Audiences?

The Corn Kings serve their clients, the government, themselves, the peasants, and their god. Their clients benefit from the low cost and high quality of their grain. The government enjoys the high taxes produced from the efficient and prosperous use of the land. The cultists build their wealth and perpetuate their life style. The peasants are provided with employment and a potent religion. Their god seems to be pleased with the bloody sacrifices and dehumanizing treatment of the laborers, and rewards the Corn Kings with bountiful crops.

Who Are the Prominent Characters?

Jaret, LE, human female, 15th level cleric (Jaret is the most influential of the Corn Kings. She is high priestess in the harvest cult and matriarch of her family.)

Typical Corn King, LE, human, 6th to 10th level cleric or wizard.

Typical Overseer, NE, human male, 5th level fighter.

Typical Zombie Worker (Corn King zombies have the statistics of common zombies, but the intelligence of juju zombies.)

The Bree

Hierarchical secret police force.

What Do They Deliver?

The Bree is a highly secretive organization of psionicists and wizards that is the secret police of the kingdom. It provides security to the king and the kingdom from internal and external threats. The members of this elite group have also built personal security and wealth by parlaying their positions into personal profit.

How Do They Acquire Resources?

This secret society is primarily funded through government taxes. The Bree has also set up a number of phony businesses and illegal operations which have generated an untold

fortune. The Bree recruits its members at an early age from the kingdom's schools.

How Are They Organized?

The Bree is organized as a rigid hierarchy with a powerful psionicist/wizard at its helm. The leader, known only as the Wraith, has direct and free access to the king.

The Bree is divided into three divisions. The largest division is the Inquisitors, who secretly collect intelligence of value to the state. The second largest division is the Readers, who analyze and compile the intelligence from the Inquisitors. The smallest group is the People's Hand. This team is responsible for planning, implementing, and controlling covert operations and counterintelligence. Any member of the Bree may commandeer the king's soldiers for any purpose, at any time.

Do They Have an Advantage?

The legal status of the members of the Bree, as well as their powerful magical and psionic abilities, allow them to freely invade the lives, minds, and property of citizens and foreigners. They usually accomplish their tasks with such secrecy that the victims are unaware of intrusion.

The Bree's existence can lead to paranoia within the state, a definite weakness that could be exploited by a clever enemy.

How Do They Plan for the Future?

The Bree has planned for its future, individually and organizationally. Members have sequestered enormous wealth used for the benefit of their retirement. They have also created imaginary threats to national security to ensure their organization's continued existence. Additionally, this group has instigated wars and treaties which it believes are in the best interest of the kingdom.

How Do They Establish Conformity?

Members of the Bree undergo intensive psionic programming and education from an early age. They maintain an intense esprit de corps. They punish transgressors in their organization by crippling offenders' mental or magical powers.

How Do They Satisfy Their Audiences?

The Bree needs to please only itself and the king. The paranoid tyrant it serves is delighted with the constant stream of information, rumor, and innuendo provided by the Bree. Members of the Bree are not entirely certain why the king does not see the group as a personal threat, but some speculate that the Wraith has more influence over the ruler than the ruler has over his land.

Who Are the Prominent Characters?

The Wraith, LE, male half-elf, 10th level psionicist/10th level wizard

Typical Inquisitor, LE, human, 6th level psionicist or wizard

Typical Reader, LE, human, 5th level psionicist or wizard

Typical People's Hand, LE, human, 8th level psionicist or wizard

The Levellers

Hierarchy of "freedom fighters," once chaotic good but now neutral evil.

What Do They Deliver?

The Levellers are an underground army of self-proclaimed freedom fighters representing an alliance of ancient clans deposed from the throne. They wage a continual war of terror against the government and populace. They deliver fear and death to their opponents, and hope and pride to their allies.

How Do They Acquire Resources?

The Levellers require funds, safe-houses, men, and weapons. They traditionally receive financial support from sympathetic freemen and contributions from families and friends. Since their campaign has become more bloody, public support for the Levellers has diminished. They have turned to robbery, blackmail, and extortion to generate income. Men are recruited from Leveller families and secretive press gangs. Weapons are purchased from black marketeers and legitimate smiths.

How Are They Organized?

The Levellers have a hierarchical cell structure, where each cell is comprised of a small team with only one point of contact to another cell. The group is headed by a charismatic fighter named Lionsburr who claims to be the heir to the throne.

Do They Have an Advantage?

The Levellers' secrecy and willingness to attack any target makes their work simple. Generations-old myths, legends, and prophecies all contribute to the group's strength.

How Do They Plan for the Future?

While the Levellers all speak of the future and their cause with the deepest conviction and highest hopes, their plans and activities do little to bring them closer to regaining the throne. Their actions increase the oppressive tactics of the government's response to their violence. Lionsburr feeds on this endless sustained conflict. He is completely taken with his own vision of the future, but would be totally unprepared if given the opportunity to rule.

How Do They Establish Conformity?

The Levellers are extremely efficient in ensuring the loyalty of their members. Any infraction or perceived doubt on the part of a Leveller is treated as treason and punished with death. Lionsburr's followers are frightened into complicity by his violence.

How Do They Satisfy Their Audiences?

The Levellers were once sensitive to public opinion and attempted to portray themselves as victims to win the favor of the mob. Lionsburr now sees the populace as ignorant children who must be beaten into obedience. The Levellers only worry about their own glorified images.

The Levellers increasing loss of public support may prove to be their downfall.

Who Are the Prominent Characters?

Lionsburr, NE, male human, 8th level fighter.

Typical Leveller, NE, human, 6th level fighter or thief.

This section serves as a source for ideas. In the beginning of this book, we established our criteria for villains. In the following chapters, we clarified and made exceptions to these rules. We now come back to the key attributes of a villain and provide ideas for you to generate your own villains.

Sources of Power

Earlier, we stated that a strong base of power to bear against the heroes was one of the requirements for an effective villain. This section describes these power bases.

Wizardly

> "I'm afraid that you'll have to come along with us," I said forcefully. The old man ignored me, looking around the floor of the cave as if he had lost something.
>
> "These bats certainly make a mess don't they?" he muttered to himself. He bent down and picked at the bat guano that was caked on the stone floor like moss. Tortle and I winced in disgust.
>
> "Come along, sir," I repeated. "We really should be going." The man scratched his finger in a yellow vein of rock—sulphur.
>
> He looked up at me. "Let me ask you, son, how far away would you say that you are standing from me? I am getting old and have difficulty seeing."
>
> "You're about fifteen feet," Tortle piped up before I could stop him. I turned my back as the old man raised a finger and shouted, "Fifteen feet!"
>
> A ball of flame engulfed us.

The most common form of power in a game is the magic of wizards. The value of magical power lies in its incredible flexibility. Some villains horde magic like a miser hordes money,

other villains want to gain magic for its own sake, while another group of villains use magic to create enough political and economic security to allow them to continue their magical research.

Wizardly power may inspire a villain with new ambitions. People often believe they could an operation more efficiently than their superiors if given the chance. One could easily imagine a wizardly counselor to a king who controls his ruler and aspires to replace him. Without the natural charisma or leadership ability of the king, the wizard would be forced to adopt tyrannical methods.

A villain does not need to be a wizard to draw upon the aid of magic. Bakshra, from the earlier examples, was a warlord who by way of alliance had access to the magical power of the wizard, Fallor. Anyone with enough money can have wizards on retainer. This can be a dangerous practice, and it would be safer for a leader to hire a handful of mid-level wizards rather than one or two powerful wizards. A single, powerful wizard would be too great a threat to a villain.

If a villain is not a mage, but makes use of complex magical defenses or tools, you should be able to logically explain how he attained his power. Make certain any associated risks are consistent with the villain's personality, and consider how this individual arranges for his security.

Clerical

> The wicked priest dropped prostrate before us. We thought he was surrendering. Then I realized he was praying.
>
> "Somebody stop him!" I bellowed. Tortle drew an arrow and fired it. The arrow missed its target and clattered across the flagstones of the temple floor. Streaks of

Clerical magic gains its power from the planes beyond the world of the player characters. Priests also acquire political, economic, and military power through the organization of their church or cult. In addition, a cleric might be able to call upon the greater power for direct intervention in his affairs. This adds an implied threat to heroes who would meddle in the affairs of an evil church.

The other interesting aspect of clerical power is the constraint it imposes upon the villain's behavior. Clerics face any number of restrictions on diet, weapons, and actions to remain in the good graces of a master. *The Complete Priest's Handbook* explains the creation of new priesthoods. When designing a cult, think about how such restrictions might make the game more interesting. What if a cultist was trying to infiltrate the party of player characters, but was required to make a blood sacrifice every day to his god? How would the villain achieve his goals without losing the god's favor?

A non-clerical villain who relies upon priests for power generally faces the same concerns as non-wizards who rely on wizards. Fortunately for the villain, priests generally act in a manner consistent with their religion. If a villain builds his power from a lawful cult, he may be exposed to less personal danger as long as his goals are consistent with those of the cult. Imagine a would-be king who promises to officially sanction an evil cult as the state religion if the priests assist in his rise to power. He might also promise to authorize a bloody inquisition to eliminate

heresy or mount a massive crusade on behalf of the cult. Occasionally, as is the case with the sorcerer-kings of Athas, a villain may actually lie at the center of the priests' cult.

Psionic

> We stood before the grand inquisitor defiantly. We had decided to teach him a lesson.
>
> "We have had enough of your harassing the people of this city. If you don't leave now, we are going to have to make you go," I announced.
>
> "Is that a fact?" the inquisitor asked. He seemed to be amused by our threats. I elbowed our mage, Zinkle.
>
> "Show him, Zinkle," I commanded.
>
> Zinkle drew a handful of powder from his pocket and began to make broad gestures. The inquisitor watched him impatiently. Zinkle suddenly paused.
>
> "Uh, wait a minute, that's not it," he mumbled, and began to gesture again for a moment before stopping it all together. He whispered nervously, "I can't remember the spell, captain."
>
> "Well, try another."
>
> "I can't remember anything. Wait, how about a trick?" he offered in vain. The inquisitor grinned and walked out.

Psionic ability has two distinct advantages. First, most players are not as familiar with psionics as they are with magic. A psionic villain is a wonderful change of pace for a psionic-poor campaign, offering a staggering variety of tools which catches most players off guard. Many psionicists' powers have effects similar to magical spells, but they cannot be detected or dispelled. A clever psionicist in a world rife with magic may have learned to disguise his methods as those of a mage.

The other interesting aspect of psionics is that most psionic abilities are available to low and mid-level psionicists. All psionicists are specialists of sorts, and they face restrictions regarding when and how they may acquire abilities outside their area of concentration. There are a number of powers with prerequisites, but few powers have level restrictions. Consequently, a fairly low-level psionicist can be a deadly specialist. A 1st level psionicist specializing in psychoportation can acquire the ability to create *dimension doors* similar to the spell which a wizard acquires at 7th level.

While psionicists are usually thought of as hermetic loners, the capability of low level psionicists to gain power quickly could provide incentive for small groups of psionicists to work together. Additionally, the psionic abilities that allow several psionicists to combine their power would give additional incentive for such a group to work together. By class restriction, psionicists are never chaotic, which makes it easier for you to build villainous organizations around psionic power.

Psionicists are usually distrusted. It is rare to find a non-psionicist depending on psionicists for their base of power. The Bene Gesserit in *Dune* were an ancient society of psionicists who advanced their own organization's agenda and insinuated themselves into affairs of state. They were rarely trusted by the villainous rulers.

When psionics is widespread, a villain may welcome such assistance. In the DARK SUN® campaign world of Athas, psionics is so widespread that no self-respecting merchant or gang leader would begin any undertaking without a psionicist's assistance. This is not motivated by a villain's love of psionicists but fear of being caught at a competitive disadvantage.

Naturally, psionics can be used to acquire other forms of power. Darth Vader gained tremendous political power from his psionic mastery. *The Complete Psionics Handbook* details all of the powers awaiting your psionic villain, and the *Dragon Kings* book describes psionic enchantment; this is a new type of power available to characters who have attained 20th level as wizards and psionicists like the sorcerer-kings of Athas.

Individual Ability (Skills)

> We looked across the room at Dirk McNasty. We were taking him in for trial.
> "Not so fast!" he barked. He quickly drew out two daggers, which he tossed from hand to hand in a dazzling but ineffective display of swordsmanship.
> "Come on, Dirk, let's go," I said growing more impatient.
> "Try this on for size!" he shouted, suddenly yanking a bell cord from the wall and tying it into a lariat. He proceeded to spin a hoop about a foot off the floor and prance in and out of the hoop as it spun. I looked at Zinkle and said, "Sleep him and let's get out of here."

While individual physical ability is often the only power available to a beginning player character, it is generally a poor base for a villain's power. Physical ability does little to mobilize an organization. Frequently, incredible Strength, an extraordinary Dexterity, or a remarkable Charisma enables a villain to accomplish great acts of treachery; bounty hunters, assassins, and mercenaries sometimes rely upon unique physical abilities. However, these individuals are unlikely to be found at the head of an organization unless they can parlay their individual abilities into some other sort of power.

A villain with little individual ability can acquire other forms of power through the extraordinary capabilities of his associates. Middlemen and brokers can act as villains, such as a carnival barker traveling with a thieving strong man, or a villain who finds mercenaries work in exchange for a cut of their fees. The personal trainer of a successful gladiator may gain political influence and wealth through the talents of his client.

Political

> When we approached the city gates, a group of guards asked us to declare any items we were planning to sell in the city. While we were explaining that we had nothing to sell and were just passing through, an elderly man in heavy robes came out of the gate house and looked us over.
> "Arrest them and hold them for further questioning," the old man ordered. He quickly returned to the gatehouse. Zinkle looked at me as if suggesting we turn and run. I shook my head.
> "That's just what they want. We have nothing to fear. We've done nothing wrong. Better go with them than never return to the city."

Political power allows a villain to muster an army, throw your player characters in prison, and pass laws that serve his personal interests. The villains with the greatest political power are often tyrants, like emperor Caligula of ancient Rome. The most dangerous political villains often operate behind a veil of legitimacy, like Prince John the usurper in the legends of Robin Hood.

Villains with a strong political power base can make great campaign villains, particularly if their power is founded in a villainous organization. This might take the form of an

evil king in control of a corrupt bureaucracy, or a member of an evil network like the Zhentarim of the FORGOTTEN REALMS® setting.

Villains may not be rulers or despots, but still have political power; any ability to get other people to perform services is a form of political power. A merchant who is able to have player characters arrested, or an innkeeper who gets the other inns in town to close their doors to the party, both have a form of political influence.

Military Power

> Bakshra's army had the city under siege for six months. Fallor's presence in the enemy command tent had prevented the church from beating back Bakshra's forces with magic. If we did not find relief, the city and the church would fall. The townspeople lost their devotion to our cause and began to look at the church as an enemy that had brought the attack upon their homes. We worried about collaborators from within and the assassins Fallor had *teleported* into the city. As we went over the day's plan of attack, Collin approached, accompanied by an imposing man in black armor.
>
> "Captain," he began. "This is a messenger from Cooldoom, the warlord of the Fallorian Alliance. He says the rest of the alliance would consider withdrawing their troops from Bakshra's siege for a price."

A long and varied history exists of villains executing plans by force of arms. Military power is usually joined with political power, and, as in the example of our siege, can quickly turn into economic power.

Military forces can be split along political lines within the same army. Ancient Rome saw it's army divided by various factions more than once. A government's police force

or military has, more than once, chosen to act independently of the government it serves.

Providing a villain with military power adds dimension and scale to any adventure. Even if the villain is a petty noble or merchant with his own private guard, the obstacles blocking the PCs' progress are immediately more challenging.

If you are interested in introducing large scale military conflicts into your game, the *AD&D*® BATTLESYSTEM® Miniatures rules and BATTLESYSTEM *Skirmishes* rules provides the game mechanics to bring them to life. *The Castle Guide* provides further insight into medieval fortresses and sieges. Even if you are not a regular player of miniatures battles, using the basic BATTLESYSTEM rules to moderate the climax of an adventure on a massive battlefield can add excitement to the game. If you take the time to familiarize yourself with the rules, you can easily coach your players through gameplay. You can have additional fun with this by allowing a guest player to run the villain's forces while you moderate combat.

Economic

> "Where is he?" I shouted. "We were supposed to interrogate him this morning, and now he's not in his cell! Who was guarding him?"
>
> "Svenson, sir," the frightened cadet answered.
>
> "Where's this Svenson?"
>
> "Missing, sir."
>
> "No sign of struggle and no sign of Svenson. I was assured the prisoner wasn't a spellcaster."
>
> "They just found Svenson, sir, and I don't think the prisoner was a spell-caster," another guard said as he entered the room.
>
> "What does that mean?" I demanded.
>
> "They found Svenson at a tavern buying drinks for the whole place. He's rich now."

Economic power ranges from the ability to control the flow of goods and services, to sheer wealth. Economic power is a versatile base for a villain; with enough money, a villain can purchase most other types of power. Likewise, an individual with some other form of power can usually use it to amass wealth.

Merchants and producers can also control the flow of goods. This power can be used to starve whole cities, drive small entrepreneurs out of business, and influence public opinion. Both the DARK SUN® and AL-QADIM® campaign worlds include merchant character classes. When creating villains whose power is based on wealth, know the origin of the wealth and how it is maintained, renewed, and increased. Many villains enter stories sitting atop massive inheritances, but the villain who has built his own wealth is more likely to have his fingers in a number of plots, with the intention of expanding his holdings.

Don't overlook the power based in the ability to control the flow of wealth. A villain can build his power base on the economic power of others with nothing more than high Charisma.

Social

> As the bard finished his performance, everyone in the theater rose to their feet and applauded. He bowed repeatedly, then waved to the crowd to take their seats. We were enjoying the brief rest from our ongoing war against Bakshra and his forces. When the crowd had quieted, the bard cleared his throat and spoke.
>
> "Good people, I thank you for your support and I very much appreciate your applause. I would like to take a moment to raise an issue that is very important to me, and because I care so much about you, I would be remiss in not mentioning it." We all listened intently.
>
> "Certain forces within our community are waging a vicious war on our neighbor to the east. I don't know much about politics, but I can tell you there are better ways to settle disagreements than at the end of a sword!" Several of the other performers stepped out onto the stage and chanted, "Stop Gonroll aggression against the Fallorian Alliance!"
>
> I slid my helmet under my seat, but it wasn't long before someone in the crowd recognized us. We ran for the side exit under a hail of vegetables and rotten fruit.

In an earlier section, we talked about public opinion as a villain. The ability to influence public opinion can be a subtle and insidious source of strength for a villain. Social power takes a variety of forms in a role-playing game; it is most dangerous when an individual can mobilize a mob against the heroes. It can be equally entertaining when an individual controls public tastes and opinion through statements or controlled public forums. Community leaders and entertainers often base their power on social influence. Villainous opinion-leaders can be seduced by the pleasure of offering their opinions, and readily volunteer them even when entirely groundless. Of course, a villainous opinion-maker can use public opinion to destroy anyone who stands in the way of his personal agenda. Like psionics, these techniques are surprisingly effective because of their infrequent use.

(Un)Natural Power

> It had been three weeks since Zinkle disappeared on his journey to find Lady Silith, the famous art dealer. He had wanted her to appraise a work of art that

had been in his family for generations. We were preparing to leave the territory and wanted Zinkle to join us.

It took about a week to catch up with Lady Silith's caravan to inquire about our friend. When we arrived, no one who worked her caravan had heard of our friend. As I continued to make inquiries, it seemed I would never find a clue to his whereabouts. On the third fruitless day with her caravan, Collin finally pulled me aside and asked, "Captain, have you looked through her sculpture tent?"

"No, Collin. Why?"

"I think you might want to take a look." I followed Collin through the statuary. He stopped at a large display of a lifelike stone statue of a man reclining in bedclothes. It was remarkable how the sculpture had captured such a realistic languid feel in stone.

I then realized the statue was Zinkle.

Your draw from the MONSTROUS COMPENDIUM® may have a host of innate powers or abilities. Powerful undead villains have devastating abilities that will set any party of heroes running. The value of such talent varies significantly among the monstrous races.

In the section "Monsters to Villains," we explained how to select a good monster for development into a villain. We looked at the importance of intelligence, social environment, and alignment. In a sense, monstrous abilities are like a villain's individual abilities in that they help the villain parlay such abilities into other forms of power. Whether this takes the form of human followers or an organization of similar creatures, a monster usually requires more than just its innate powers to become a master villain.

However, as we mentioned in the section on individual ability, lone professionals often become formidable villains either on their own or in the service of an organization.

Some monsters would do well as thieves, bounty-hunters, or assassins if they have the inclination and can find the work. Dopplegangers have hired out as assassins.

Interesting alliances can arise between mundane but ambitious villains who can strike alliances with monstrous creatures. Like a fighter who hires a wizard, these alliances can result in the ultimate undoing of the villain as easily as they can result in his or her advancement. Fzoul Chembryl, the high priest of Bane at Zhentil Keep in the FORGOTTEN REALMS® setting has, to his advantage, made an ally of Xulla, the beholder. On the other hand, Faust and Melmoth (among others) were destroyed by their evil alliances with malign entities.

Bad Objectives

For game purposes, an objective is the goal which turns your villain's need into a plot. The following is a list of possible goals you can use to develop an adventure. Each goal listed here includes a number of possible plot ideas which the goal might inspire.

Immortality

• A wizard attempts to become a lich and hires a party to collect crucial components.

• A warlord imprisons a sorcerer and demands that to obtain his freedom he must develop the magic necessary to confer immortality. A party is hired to free the wizard.

• A party is called to prevent a ritual in which a dark priest of an evil god plans to achieve deification.

• An aging king seeks the company of vampires to gain immortality. The king's daughter hires a party to foil his plan.

Wealth

- A doppleganger decides to enjoy the wealth of one of its victims. The victim's heir suspects something unusual when his "father" suddenly changes his will. The party is hired to investigate.

- A secret society is founded to make money through extortion, and enforces its authority by assassination and murder. A businessman who is a friend of the adventurers falls prey to this villainous organization.

- A charming suitor pursues marriage with a wealthy PC, planning to kill the PC and seize the fortune.

- A local constable frames a poor farmer for murder to acquire his land. The PCs are hired by the constable to help convict and evict the farmer.

Military/Political Power

- The disinherited son of the king vows to take the throne. The PCs are hired by the king's appointed heir to stop the rival.

- A general to a tyrannical king organizes a faction of the army to overthrow the government. He hires the PCs to assist in his campaign of "liberation," but reveals himself to be as brutal as the current ruler. The conflict may succeed in starting a civil war.

- A group of corrupt merchants put forward a candidate for public office. The incumbent hires the PCs to collect intelligence on his opposition.

- A political party terrorizes the populace to remain in power. The PCs are asked to join an underground alliance to destabilize the power.

Magical Power

- A fraternity of religious fanatics with a long history of bloody sacrifices plunder their victims' property to provide their economic support. A victim's relatives hire the PCs to infiltrate the organization to discover a way to destroy it.

- A wizard summons an extraplanar being. The creature breaks free of its master's control, and the wizard hires the PCs to stop it.

- An evil cleric is driven to gain magical power to raise his wife from the dead. The woman's father hires the PCs to stop him.

- A psionicist gains the power to control people's thoughts. The PCs stumble across his town, where he holds the entire population under his influence. The free thoughts of the party attract the attention of the villain.

Revenge

- The PCs are hired to protect the last heir of a noble family under the curse of a dwarf who was refused shelter decades earlier.

- A villain who has been imprisoned for years escapes and vows revenge upon the sentencing judge. The PCs are hired by the constable who originally captured the villain to track him down before he reaches the judge.

- A bitter fighter wants to exterminate all halflings for having killed his father.

- A halfling PC becomes the target of a fighter's enmity.

- A bard is attempting to poison townspeople for having laughed him off stage.

Self-Aggrandizement

- A villain kills a popular leader to gain a reputation as a master assassin. The PCs are hired to bring him to justice.

- The PCs are invited to participate in a tournament which a jealous knight sabotages to gain victory. The knight, however, is very popular with the king.

- A young group of adventurers plan to kill the PCs to make their reputation as formidable mercenaries.

- Two powerful wizards agree to meet in a small town to duel for the title of Conjurer Supreme. The town fears destruction and hires the PCs to convince the wizards to cancel the contest. Failing this, the wizards are to be captured or slain.

Love

- A young woman insists her lover perform crimes of increasing savagery to prove his love. The adventurers are hired by the town council to investigate the mysterious acts of mayhem.

- Embittered after being jilted by a beautiful princess, a knight kidnaps her and holds her for ransom. The unwitting PCs are hired by the knight to escort his bride-to-be through hostile territory.

- In pursuit of love, a young wizard *charms* and enslaves an entire town. The PCs are hired to break the enchantment and free the community. But everyone *loves* the wizard, so . . .

- A monster falls in love with a PC and kills anyone who gets near her.

Bad Motives

When we defined a villain at the beginning of this book, we explained that bad motives are the essence of villainy. We also said that a bad motive was any need pursued at the expense of others' welfare.

Each of the needs below is described in the section on "Defining a Villain." Any of these will serve as a motive for your villain.

Achievement	Nurturing
Affiliation	Order
Aggression	Power
Autonomy	Succor
Exhibition	Understanding
Safety	

Bad Personality

Below are some personality traits and character flaws that can be used as the fundamental weakness of a villain. The *DMG* provides a table for randomly generating a non-player character's personality, which you can also use to generate ideas for your villain's personality. A villain does not need to have an offensive personality to be an effective villain; some of the great villains of literature have been extremely polite or charming people. However, poor character makes a villain more unsympathetic, which is essential to any good adversary. When providing a villain with a contradictory trait, remember that the intention is to make him more interesting, not more sympathetic.

Arrogant

Excessive pride, lack of humility or the failure to see the limit of one's abilities. Arrogance often results in the villain's attempts to usurp power, and is often veiled under for-

mal politeness. The arrogant belief of Dr. Frankenstein that he could create life created a series of tragedies ultimately ending in his death, as well as that of his creature.

Avaricious

Extremely greedy and stingy, with no ambition or principle beyond the hoarding of money. In order to satisfy his passion for riches, a person may turn to a life of crime. Goldfinger, the gold-smuggling villain in the Ian Fleming book of the same name, is driven to commit unthinkable crimes in pursuit of his desperate desire for more gold.

Compulsive/Obsessive

To have an irresistible impulse. Bakshra, our villain in the second chapter of this book, is a compulsive man who makes a ritual of eating dog meat every evening. Bakshra is also inordinately attentive to his health.

Cruel/Sadistic

Pitiless and harsh, deliberately causing others to suffer and delighting in the cruelty. This is a common characteristic of villains. Nurse Ratched in *One Flew Over the Cuckoo's Nest* humiliates and mistreats her patients. The Marquis de St. Evremonde in Dickens' *Tale of Two Cities* runs over a child with his coach without remorse. In the movie *Marathon Man*, the villain tortures his victim with a dentist's drill, without anesthetic.

Duplicitous

Treacherous, deceitful, and unfaithful, a despicable flaw. Benedict Arnold was a remarkable soldier during the American Revolution, but when he became commander of West Point he plotted with the English for its takeover. The treason was exposed, and Arnold joined the British army. He was despised, even by the English people, for his betrayal.

Nihilistic

Total denial of principles or institutions valued by society. A nihilist believes no cause is worthy of action; it is evil in the form of emptiness. In the *Odyssey*, the Lotus Eaters tempted the men of Odysseus to give up their search for their homeland and loved ones.

Envious

Resentment over the success or possessions of another. In *Wuthering Heights*, Hindley has an immediate jealous hatred of an abandoned child, Heathcliff, brought home by his father. This jealousy increases over the years and results in misfortune.

Gluttonous

Epicurean, sensualist, or devoted to luxurious living that satisfies appetites at the expense of everything else. The Roman Emperor Caligula's pursuit of lavish and elegant absurdities led to problems in the empire and his eventual assassination.

Insane

Madness, lunacy, one who behaves irrationally. A person who is insane is frightening and can be a fun villain. In Hitchcock's *Psycho*, Norman Bates is the classic psychotic villain. Alex in *Fatal Attraction* is another example of neurosis in action. A sociopath or psychopath can be a fearless and unpredictable villain. But remember, these charac-

ters are generally static: They do not have the ability to transform or develop.

Intelligent

A strong or brilliant mind. Cunning genius can be villainous when used for diabolical purposes. Fu Manchu used his intelligence to plan cruel deaths for those who stepped in the way of his ambitions.

Deceptive

Liars, false prophets, hypocrites and oath-breakers given to untruth and deception. One who feigns virtuous qualities. The cult leader Jim Jones convinced his followers of his divinity and led them to their deaths. Moliere's villain Tartufe disguises himself with a mask of piety and connives a wealthy merchant to give him property and his daughter's hand in marriage.

Lustful

Excessive sexual appetite. A foul witch may assume the form of a beautiful princess to entice a knight into her lair. The daughter-in-law of the farm owner in *Of Mice and Men* seduces Lennie, the half-wit. Her flaw leads to her own death, as well as Lennie's.

Manipulative

To manipulate the perceptions of others for one's own benefit. The truth-shaper or spin doctor. The Bene Gesserit in Frank Herbert's *Dune* manipulated marriages to ensure the birth of their messiah.

Opportunistic

To use every available opportunity to achieve one's goal without regard for morality or sentiment. In 17th-century England, Jonathan Wild incited robbery, informed on the thieves, claimed the reward, and watched them march to the gallows.

Slothful

Lazy and habitually indolent. A slothful villain can be dangerous when others are relying on him to perform some critical action. Laziness often leads to negligence.

Vain

Excessive conceit. The evil queen in *Snow White* is so distraught by Snow White's greater beauty that she plots the girl's death.

Vindictive

To seek retribution for a wrong. In *Arabian Nights,* the sultan vows to marry a lady every day and have her head cut off the next morning to avenge himself for the disloyalty of his first wife.

Intolerant

Irrational suspicion or hatred of a particular group, race, or religion. History abounds with intolerant villains whose prejudice resulted in the suffering of innocents.

Selfish

Concerned only with oneself, egocentric and egoistic. Selfishness is practically a prerequisite for a villain. Some historians attribute the decline of the Roman Empire to emperors who were concerned only with their own pleasure and glory.

Villain Tables

These tables have been provided to help you randomly generate ideas for villains. The General Traits Table from the *DMG* has also been included to give you some ideas for additional personality traits. This chart can be particularly helpful when trying to find a contradictory personality trait for your villain.

Table 1: Bad Methods (1d100)

While most villains want to maintain an outward appearance of respectability, many resort to despicable tactics to advance their interests. This list catalogs some particularly nasty acts or unusual practices that can heighten the players' fear and loathing of your villain.

01	Acid
02	Adultery
03	Ambush
04	Arson
05	Assassination
06	Assault/beatings
07	Beheading
08	Betrayal/treason
09	Blackmail/extortion
10	Blights/crop failures
11	Blinding
12	Bounty hunting
13	Branding
14	Breach of contract
15	Bribery
16	Burglary/theft
17	Burning at the stake
18	Burying alive
19	Cannibalism
20	Charms
21	Cheating
22	Confidence scams
23	Conspiracy
24	Counterfeiting
25	Crucifixion
26	Curses
27	Desecration
28	Dismemberment
29	Drawing and quartering
30	Drought/famine
31	Drowning
32	Drugs/alcohol
33	Dueling
34	Electrocution
35	Espionage/spying
36	Euthanasia, involuntary
37	Eviction
38	Execution, general
39	Fast-talking
40	Fine print
41	Flaying
42	Fortune-telling

43	Framing
44	Fraud/swindling
45	Gambling
46	Garroting/suffocation
47	Genocide
48	Gossiping/slander
49	Hanging
50	Hauntings
51	Heresy/cults
52	Humiliation
53	Idolatry/false gods
54	Illusions
55	Impalement
56	Impersonation/disguise
57	Imprisonment
58	Invasion/warfare
59	Kidnapping
60	Lechery
61	Legal intimidation
62	Libel/insults
63	Looting
64	Lying/perjury
65	Massacres
66	Mercenaries
67	Missiles
68	Mugging
69	Murder, general
70	Neglect
71	Oppression
72	Petrification
73	Plagues/disease
74	Poaching
75	Poisoning
76	Press gangs
77	Psionics, baneful
78	Quackery/tricks
79	Racking
80	Raising taxes
81	Raising the dead
82	Rebellion
83	Sacrifice, live
84	Scalping
85	Seduction
86	Seizing property
87	Selling their souls
88	Setting traps
89	Shackling
90	Slavery
91	Smuggling
92	Spells, baneful
93	Stabbing
94	Stalking
95	Summoning monsters
96	Terrorism
97	Threats/harassment
98	Thumbscrews
99	Torture, general
100	Whipping

Table 2:
Source of Power (1d10)
1. Wizardly Magic
2. Clerical Magic
3. Psionics
4. Individual Ability
5. Political Capital
6. Military Strength
7. Economic Resources
8. Social Influence
9. Unnatural Power
10. Roll Again

Table 3:
Bad Objectives (1d8)
1. Immortality
2. Wealth
3. Military Power
4. Political Power
5. Magical Power
6. Revenge
7. Self-Aggrandizement
8. Love

Table 4:
Bad Motives (1d12)
1. Achievement
2. Affiliation
3. Aggression
4. Autonomy
5. Exhibition
6. Safety
7. Nurturing
8. Order
9. Power
10. Succor
11. Understanding
12. Roll Again

Table 5:
Bad Personality (1d20)
1. Arrogant
2. Avaricious
3. Compulsive/Obsessive
4. Cruel/Sadistic
5. Duplicitous
6. Nihilistic
7. Envious
8. Gluttonous
9. Insane
10. Intelligent
11. Deceptive
12. Lustful
13. Manipulative
14. Opportunistic
15. Slothful
16. Vain
17. Vindictive
18. Intolerant
19. Selfish
20. Roll Again

Table 6: GENERAL TRAITS

Die Roll 1 (d20)	General Trait	Die Roll 2 (%)	Specific Trait	Die Roll 1 (d20)	General Trait	Die Roll 2 (%)	Specific Trait	Die Roll 1 (d20)	General Trait	Die Roll 2 (%)	Specific Trait
1	Argumentative			7	Exacting			14	Optimistic		
		01	Garrulous			31	Perfectionist			66	Cheerful
		02	Hot-tempered			32	Stern			67	Happy
		03	Overbearing			33	Harsh			68	Diplomatic
		04	Articulate			34	Punctual			69	Pleasant
		05	Antagonistic			35	Driven			70	Foolhardy
2	Arrogant			8	Friendly			15	Pessimistic		
		06	Haughty			36	Trusting			71	Fatalistic
		07	Elitist			37	Kind-hearted			72	Depressing
		08	Proud			38	Forgiving			73	Cynical
		09	Rude			39	Easy-going			74	Sarcastic
		10	Aloof			40	Compassionate			75	Realistic
3	Capricious			9	Greedy			16	Quiet		
		11	Mischievous			41	Miserly			76	Laconic
		12	Impulsive			42	Hard-headed			77	Soft-spoken
		13	Lusty			43	Covetous			78	Secretive
		14	Irreverent			44	Avaricious			79	Retiring
		15	Madcap			45	Thrifty			80	Mousy
4	Careless			10	Generous			17	Sober		
		16	Thoughtless			46	Wastrel			81	Practical
		17	Absent-minded			47	Spendthrift			82	Level-headed
		18	Dreamy			48	Extravagant			83	Dull
		19	No common sense			49	Kind			84	Reverent
		20	Insensitive			50	Charitable			85	Ponderous
5	Courage			11	Moody			18	Suspicious		
		21	Brave			51	Gloomy			86	Scheming
		22	Craven			52	Morose			87	Paranoid
		23	Shy			53	Compulsive			88	Cautious
		24	Fearless			54	Irritable			89	Deceitful
		25	Obsequious			55	Vengeful			90	Nervous
6	Curious			12	Naive			19	Uncivilized		
		26	Inquisitive			56	Honest			91	Uncultured
		27	Prying			57	Truthful			92	Boorish
		28	Intellectual			58	Innocent			93	Barbaric
		29	Perceptive			59	Gullible			94	Graceless
		30	Keen			60	Hick			95	Crude
				13	Opinionated			20	Violent		
						61	Bigoted			96	Cruel
						62	Biased			97	Sadistic
						63	Narrow-minded			98	Immoral
						64	Blustering			99	Jealous
						65	Hide-bound			00	Warlike